CURSE OF THE
NIGHT WITCH

CURSE OF THE
NIGHT WITCH

EMBLEM ISLAND

BOOK 1

ALEX ASTER

sourcebooks
young readers

Copyright © 2020 by Alex Aster
Cover and internal design © 2020 by Sourcebooks
Cover art © Fiona Hsieh/Shannon Associates
Internal design by Danielle McNaughton
Internal images © Shutterstock

Sourcebooks and the colophon are registered trademarks of Sourcebooks.

Published by Sourcebooks Young Readers, an imprint of Sourcebooks Kids
P.O. Box 4410, Naperville, Illinois 60567-4410
(630) 961-3900
sourcebookskids.com

Library of Congress Cataloging-in-Publication Data

Names: Aster, Alex, author.
Title: Curse of the Night Witch / Alex Aster.
Description: Naperville, IL : Sourcebooks Young Readers, [2020] | Series:
    Emblem Island ; book 1 | Audience: Ages 8-14. | Audience: Grades 4-6. |
    Summary: After changing the fate he has known since birth,
    twelve-year-old Tor Luna, accompanied by his friends Engle and Melda,
    must visit the notorious Night Witch to break the curse he now faces.
Identifiers: LCCN 2019052808 | (hardcover)
Subjects: CYAC: Fate and fatalism–Fiction. | Blessing and
    cursing–Fiction. | Quests (Expeditions)–Fiction. | Witches–Fiction. |
    Fantasy.
Classification: LCC PZ7.1.A882 Cur 2020 | DDC [Fic]–dc23
LC record available at https://lccn.loc.gov/2019052808

This product conforms to all applicable CPSC and CPSIA standards.

Source of Production: Maple Press, York, Pennsylvania, United States
Date of Production: March 2020
Run Number: 5017863

Printed and bound in the United States of America.
MA 10 9 8 7 6 5 4 3 2 1

To JonCarlos and Luna.

And to my grandma, who told me the story

of the girl with the star on her forehead.

CURSE OF THE
NIGHT WITCH

1

THE WISH

Tor Luna often studied his little sister's lifeline. Today he ran a finger across Rosa's tiny hands, and she squirmed, laughing. "Look at all of those peaks," he said, tapping the rainbow-colored lines winding up and down her palms.

"More than the Scalawag Range, even," Rosa said with a smug grin. She had never seen the Scalawag Range, Tor knew—and neither had he. But the famous mountains were rumored to dwarf the ones that surrounded their village like fences.

He closed Rosa's hand gently with his own, satisfied. Though it was rare, lifelines could change overnight, so Tor always checked, just in case. He found the ritual comforting. Seeing Rosa's destiny printed out in front of him, across both palms, was like witnessing her future unfold: the challenges (valleys), the trials (loops), and, of course, the accomplishments (peaks). Her lifeline was longer than average, dipping down almost all the way to her right wrist. And Tor was grateful for that.

His mother was most grateful of all. Eight years earlier, the day Rosa was born, Chieftess Luna had studied the little girl's hands and breathed a sigh of relief. Then, surrounded by all of their village and the hollow echo of beating drums, the Chieftess had carefully examined every inch of her newborn, searching for an emblem. The crowd moved like a wave— rocking forward in anticipation, their sharp whispers like cracks of fire. The Chieftess had not needed to look for long.

"There!" Tor yelled, pointing at his little sister's throat.

A small red heart sat on the left side of her neck, directly between her jaw and collarbone. Tor's mother smiled, and the crowd cooed approvingly. "A singer," she said, pressing a gentle finger to the baby's skin.

It was a good gift. Not as rare as others, but a good emblem nonetheless. Some were born with nothing at all, the Chieftess was quick to remind her children. *Markless*, they were called.

"More than the Scalawag Range," Tor repeated with a small smile, then shot a glance at his own hands. Just like Rosa, his lifeline had never changed.

Sometimes, he wished it would.

The colorful lines on his palms ran steadily—*boringly*—straight. No high peaks, or even low valleys, to speak of. "A nice, comfortable life," his mother liked to say, her eyes smiling like that was a good thing.

Tor was always very quick to point out that it was not. A steady lifeline meant no pain or complications, that was true. But it also meant nothing to look forward to. No adventure.

What was life without a dash of danger?

There was *one* thing out of the ordinary about Tor's lifeline, however. A tiny knot on his left hand, where all of the lines tied together in a small speck of a twist. It was so tiny, so unnoticeable, that the village's elderly palm reader had squinted at it, glasses perched on the second bump of her nose, and shrugged. "I don't see any knot," she had declared.

But Tor saw it. And he hoped that it meant something.

A sliver of pink swirled across the sky, and Rosa's dark brown eyes widened. "I'm late!" she yelled, running out of their home, built, like all of the others, into the base of a large tree.

Tor sighed. Rosa was always late, and she always looked surprised about it.

Moments later, a perfect melody broke through the dawn. A chorus of voices that never cracked or faltered were performing their morning song. There was shuffling outside as the village woke up, each member shedding layers of sleep, dreams, and possibly nightmares.

The tune went on, then seamlessly transitioned into a simple song only performed once every twelve months, on New Year's Eve. The island's most important holiday.

Each new year was a new opportunity to make a wish—and the Emblemites wrote theirs on leaves. On the night of December 31, each desire was thrown into a glorious bonfire.

A wish was a sacred thing. It had to be born from the heart of true desire. And there were rules. No vengeance or violence allowed. And there were *risks*. Crafting bad wishes could end in the wisher being cursed.

And, as with all things, there was luck. Of the many wishes submitted, only a few of the island's inhabitants would find theirs granted in the new year, along with a gold star on their skin, to remind them of the gift they were given.

Tor had written his own wish months before and had carried the worn leaf in his pocket ever since...waiting. Hearing the Eve song finally playing, he smiled and danced his fingers across it.

Today's the day, today's the day, today's the day, he chanted in his head until the words bled together.

"Happy day," his mother said from behind him. Tor jumped, quickly pulling his hand from his pocket.

4

He nodded in response, then walked toward the kitchen, mumbling about finding their tin of canela tea. Just then, his father walked in, holding a tray with four clay mugs of the traditional Eve drink. Of course he'd already made it. His talent was cooking, and he had the knife symbol on his index finger to prove it.

"Happy Eve," his father said, planting a kiss on top of Tor's head.

Tor smiled, but only one side of his mouth pulled up. His father eyed him for a few moments too long. Could he tell that Tor was sweating? Was his wish sticking out of his pocket?

Then, his father smiled back. At the same moment, Rosa crashed through the front door, black braids swinging behind her. She was humming a tune as sweet as emerald pudding, soft as the gentle ping of wind chimes. Tor's parents looked at each other in a loving way that made him half nauseated and half happy.

"School," he mumbled, grabbing his lunch pack and heading out of the kitchen.

His mother's head turned with hawk-like speed. "This early?"

Why couldn't his mother be bad at her job, just this once? Care just a little less? He wouldn't mind having an absentee mom; his friend Engle turned out just fine without having *his*

5

parents around all the time. Tor swallowed and tried not to look at his feet. That would certainly give him away. "Leadership board meets before class starts."

He froze, waiting for his mother's eyebrows to twist in suspicion. But that didn't happen. She smiled, and her eyes filled with something dangerous—hope. Tor felt a knife of guilt twist in his stomach.

His mother's smile dropped as quickly as it had formed. "Go on, then," she said calmly, like she believed that sounding too excited would make Tor suddenly realize he did not, in fact, want to be on leadership board.

He backed out of the room, then ran out of the house, carefully closing the heavy front door behind him. Nervous sweat spotted his forehead as a few leaves sprinkled down from the branches that stretched above his home like welcoming arms. The leaves were purple. A powerful color, the shade of a Chieftess. Tor swallowed. He didn't like the color at all, or what it symbolized. Unfortunately, he had the hue printed right on his skin. Two purple rings around his left wrist.

Tor took one look at his leadership emblem and wondered if his mother would ever forgive him for what he was going to do.

The Charmed Necklace

Once upon a shooting star, a girl named Estrelle was given a necklace by her grandmother. It looked like a bubble and held tiny charms, crafted from glittering gems.

That same day her grandmother put her into a boat and pushed it out to sea. The war had found their home, and escape was the only hope of living another day. Estrelle screamed for her grandmother to join her, but she could not.

So Estrelle floated through the ocean with just her necklace, a canteen of water, and a single bag of food for ten days and ten nights.

She was asleep, curled up in the small boat, when its bottom dragged roughly ashore.

This was a very different land from the one she had left. The sea held just a hint of blue. The beach was a stretch of gray.

Estrelle held her necklace tightly in her palm as she took her first step onto her new home.

The rest of the island was just as plain. Trees wore

pale leaves that fell easily with the wind, and the dirt was too dry, like the ash from her family's hearth. Plants grew folded over, if at all. Fruits were born spoiled.

She fought to survive in this soulless wild, filled with colorless animals and fanged, frightening beasts. Each day was harder than the last, the land barren, as if a storm had ripped right through it, taking all of the good parts for itself.

For a while, Estelle roamed the island as though she were a ghost trapped among ruins, never speaking and forcing her memories away, knowing such happiness was not welcomed in such a gray place. Until one night, when she looked up at the sky and finally cried, missing her old life...wondering if her grandmother had survived. And, if she hadn't, if she was looking down upon her.

A tear fell upon her necklace; the glass cracked, and the rainbow charm fell onto her arm.

She watched in awe as the charm sank into her skin, printed there forever. When Estrelle touched a finger to the ground, it exploded in glorious green.

When she dipped her hand into the ocean, blue spiraled through the waves, until the entire sea glowed lapis lazuli. Everything she touched, from the fruits, to the trees, to the animals, to the beasts, were gifted color...until she had painted all of the island to her liking.

When, months later, she happened upon other inhabitants on the far side of the island, she gave them each one of her magical charms, understanding very well that she could not wear them all.

A fish, for one who found he could breathe underwater.

A moon, for another who discovered she could control the sea.

And a tiger, for a girl who found she could speak to animals.

Before long, children were born with their own markings, and the original necklace was lost to time.

And so emblems began.

2

EVE

The beach was empty, save for three noisy, single-legged birds that hopped about and a mess of giant pale shells, waiting to be collected by villagers hoping to find equally large pearls inside. The tops of the shells were starting to gray, which meant they were ripe and ready to be cracked open.

Tor flung off his shoes, socks, and school uniform with relief. When he was down to his swim trunks, the first rays of the day's sun danced across his tanned arms, down his back, all the way to his toes, which he curled into the damp sand.

It was a routine he had practiced for years: sneaking out at night or early in the morning, taking back roads so no one in the village would see him making his way to the ocean, just to swim. He had become an expert at walking quietly on the tips of his toes, stepping on the floorboards in his house that didn't creak, and ducking underneath candlelit windows.

A wave dove forward, and Tor raced to meet it, a chill pirouetting down his spine as the water worked its way through his dark hair. He moved his legs and arms in sync—forward, out, and back—just like he had seen frogs do when he was younger. He cut through the sea quickly, not only to get to his favorite reef, but also to rid himself of anger and frustration that only seemed to disappear when he swam. The water absorbed it all, taking his worries and fears and beating them until they were smooth as his father's whipped cream. He kept going until his limbs were limp with fatigue and relief.

Only then did he take a deep breath and let himself sink.

A stream of bubbles trailed out of his mouth as he descended to the ocean floor. Eyes closed, faraway ringing in his ears, he felt completely at peace.

His grandfather used to speak of the calming effects of meditation, along with the benefits of eating raw grass, which, Tor admitted, made anything else he said a bit less credible. Still—though it made Tor cringe to think he had much in common with his strange grandpa—swimming was, in a way, *his* meditation...the only time he felt completely whole.

Completely happy.

He thanked the wish-gods that he lived near such a

glorious sea. The ocean off the village of Estrelle was famous, mostly because many of the sea creatures that lived there had gigantism. Starfish the size of rugs carpeted the seafloor in shades that ranged from purple to gold, and large shells often produced pearls so big they would have to be carried inland by five villagers with a net. He had even seen a crab with claws like tree trunks once.

But it was also glorious because Sapphire Sea was indeed sapphire blue—a hue that seemed unnaturally bright, too pigmented to exist. He had only ever seen the rich color one other place: in the eyes of a classmate he didn't particularly care for.

When Tor finally reached the bottom, he blinked.

Maybe it was because he was used to it, after swimming every day for most of his life, or maybe it was something else entirely, but Tor didn't feel the sting of salt in his eyes. He watched the ocean world as easily as he watched life on land, and he could swallow a mouthful of seawater without feeling a single twinge in his throat.

It wasn't normal, he knew, not to be bothered by the salt. His friend Engle never went in the ocean for that exact reason; his eyes *were* more sensitive than most. On the mornings Engle joined Tor on the beach, Engle would forgo swimming entirely, instead climbing to the top of a palm tree to use his emblem to watch out for sharks and man-eating squids.

Though his own eyes remained unbothered, Tor *did* feel the shudder of his lungs that meant he had been underwater too long. Still, he stayed, studying the bouquets of coral to his left. Spike, a red sea urchin Tor had watched grow from just a speck into the size of a human head, had moved, and now sat underneath the shadow of a veiny sea fan. Engle said Spike would live a hundred years, which Tor wouldn't have believed if anyone else had told him so. But Engle knew more about the creatures of Emblem Island than even Theodora, a girl in their year whose emblem allowed her to talk to animals.

Something in his chest contracted; his lungs officially felt like they were shriveling into raisins. Begrudgingly, Tor kicked off from the bottom, foot barely missing a starfish, shooting for the surface and gasping for air as he finally broke through.

Hair plastered to his forehead, Tor took five big breaths. After years of swimming, he had turned it into a sort of science. Five full breaths equaled approximately two good minutes underwater.

He was back in business.

This time, though, Tor dove forward, not down. He was going to the Bone Boat.

A hundred years before, a ship carrying enchanted objects sank just short of reaching shore. Before learning how to evade a shark, and even before being taught how to swim free of a riptide, Tor knew that touching the Bone Boat's treasure was strictly forbidden. Doing so would unleash a fury-storm of repercussions: a hundred years of curses, teeth falling from the sky, the sea turning gray, blah blah blah, the same old tales Tor liked to roll his eyes at.

Still, no one had said anything about *looking* at the boat—omens and foreboding didn't exactly have fine print. So, Tor swam down the mast, all the way to the deck, where all of the enchanted items had come to rest, covered in ribbon-like seaweed and mossy algae.

That's when he saw it. The gleam of something silver. Something tucked beneath a dislodged board.

It looked like a ring. No, possibly a pin. A coin?

If only he could hold it, just to see what it could do. No one would know... He could simply reach down and grab it.

No. He stopped himself, barely.

Even though Tor didn't necessarily believe in curses, mostly because he'd never heard of any actually happening outside of lore, he didn't exactly want to be the one to test if the stories were true.

So, with a bubble-trail sigh, he turned around and decided to collect shells instead. For half an hour, he floated on his stomach, eyes trained on the ocean floor, looking for the sparkle of a particularly nice one. He waited patiently, watching the current shift the sand—and like a blanket being pulled away, an entirely new array of shells was revealed. Then, he dove down to collect the ones he liked best before the sand could reclaim them.

This time, when Tor went for another breath of air, the sky had changed. It had gone from dawn's light pink to morning's blue, which meant it was time for school.

He released the fistful of shells he had found down to the seafloor, a lightning bolt of disappointment running through his stomach as he watched them go. Still, he knew he couldn't keep them. Of course he couldn't. Engle was the only one who knew Tor still swam.

Ever since his teacher had sent a letter home detailing his lack of work ethic—or, more accurately, lack of work *period*— Tor's parents had made it abundantly clear he had to focus solely on his training from then on.

Which, unfortunately, did not involve water.

He dragged his feet on his way to shore. Sun burning the top of his head, Tor squeezed the ends of his swim trunks dry, then got dressed. Without a towel to use—which definitely would have aroused suspicion—his socks ended up caked in sand and the very tips of his shoes held sloshing water. But he didn't mind. No, he *liked* it. Ground-up shell between his toes made eight hours of class seem almost bearable.

Azulmar Academy was built right into the side of a mountain students called Point, since its peak resembled an arrowhead. The school's back walls were a sparkling gray granite, and large fires burned in the main hall, visible from the always-open, colossus-sized front doors. It looked rather warm and welcoming.

The teachers, however, did not.

"Boy!" A thunderous voice came out of a woman barely four feet tall. Students liked to joke that Mrs. Alma had some gnome in her bloodline, but they weren't serious. Everyone knew gnomes had gone extinct long ago, in the last ice age. Engle swore he saw a frozen one once, at a market in the city of Zeal.

Tor swallowed. "Yes, Mrs. Alma?"

She pointed her disturbingly long, curved fingernail at him and wagged it back and forth the way a dog might move its tail under happier circumstances. "Went and ran off early yesterday, did you? Left three entire pamphlets unread!" Mrs. Alma had terrible eyesight and a habit of losing her glasses, so it was usually pretty easy to skip out on work. When Tor wasn't running off to the beach, he was daydreaming about it.

At Azulmar, a student only studied that which was relevant to their emblems—their gifts.

And Tor hated his.

If anyone took a look at his daily schedule, he was pretty sure they wouldn't blame him. As a natural-born leader, like his mother, Tor's lessons consisted of studying years' worth of past political events, documents, and decisions. Not only were these papers long, but the people with leadership emblems never seemed to be good writers, which meant countless hours of reading sentences that never seemed to end, and about events that were more boring than stale bread.

Really, though, it wouldn't have mattered if his classes were as thrilling as those of the elixir students, who spent their days stirring bubbling chemical concoctions. *Any* ability unrelated to water didn't interest Tor in the slightest. Swimming was the only thing he had ever been passionate about.

To make matters worse, his emblem's class was the smallest in the school. There were just two of them.

She, at least, seemed to like the subject matter.

Melda Alexander came skipping through the school's front doors. "Not to worry, Mrs. Alma. I'll give Tor my outline of the chapters he missed."

Mrs. Alma turned to face Melda, but stopped about ten degrees too short, making it look like she was addressing one of the gray gargoyles that flanked Azulmar's entrance. Her expression changed completely. "That's very kind of you."

17

Mrs. Alma favored Melda more than any of her other students. Maybe more than anyone ever. The woman turned vaguely in Tor's direction. "Don't let it happen again," she said, then shuffled away, grumbling.

Tor sighed and faced Melda. "Thanks."

She squinted her sapphire eyes at him. Blue was an extremely rare eye color, and Tor thought it was wasted on someone as snobby as her. "Just to be clear, I'm only helping you because I don't want any bad karma affecting my Eve wish," she said, before gripping the pendant she always wore between her fingers and turning on her heel toward class.

Lessons that day were the same as every day before. In the six years Tor had been doing leadership training, he spent most of his time alternating between pretending to read and staring at the clock, wishing he had an hourglass emblem so that he could make the timepiece's hands move to noon with his mind.

But Tor had a plan that he hoped would change every-thing. He looked down at the emblem wrapped around his left wrist and smiled. With any luck, he would be free of it by the next day.

The moment Tor spotted Engle in the lunchroom, his best friend said, "Did you really bring your wish to school?"

Tor gulped, his hand instinctively moving to his pocket.

Engle caught his sudden movement and raised his eyebrows, clearly curious.

"Well?" Engle asked, sitting across from him at their usual lunch table. Most of the school sat with their emblem groups, but Tor and Engle had been best friends for as long as they could remember, so they always sat together.

Engle had the gift of sightseeing, which meant he could spot a marble from a mile away—or a shark speeding through the depths of Sapphire Sea. Sometimes, when the weather was right, and his eyes weren't itchy, he could even see *through* objects. Luckily for Tor, his see-through vision was still a little blurry.

Tor sighed and bent his head down low. "Yes. Don't try to read it."

Engle nodded. A wish revealed was a wish ungranted. Everyone knew that.

"Well, *my* wish is safe, back at home, where no one will find it, right underneath my hydroclops statue," Engle said. He froze and laughed nervously, looking like he wished he could take back his last few words. "Um, don't tell anyone that."

Tor was curious at what Engle would want to wish for. As far as he could tell, his friend was happy.

"Secret's safe with me," Tor said.

"And with me." The voice came from behind them, and

they both startled, whipping around to see who had been snooping on their conversation.

Of course. Melda.

Engle's shoulders tensed, then he rolled his eyes. "Should have seen her coming," he mumbled.

"Yes, *Grimelda*?" Tor asked. Everyone called her Melda, but Engle had spotted her full name once on paperwork in the main office from all the way down the hallway, and Tor liked to use it when she was being especially annoying.

Her eyes squinted into a glare. "Just wanted to drop these off," she said, leaving a stack of papers in front of him. Tor blinked. Her supposed outlines looked *longer* than the treatises themselves.

Then she made her way back to her table, books stacked where Tor should probably have been.

●) ◗ ☾

One of Tor's favorite parts about Eve was that class let out early. He hummed happily as he walked up and down the three hills between Azulmar and the village. Rosa was far ahead, walking with the other chorus members. Engle, who was likely zooming and unzooming his vision for fun, was by his side.

Their town was one of many that existed on Emblem

Island. It was named Estrelle after the person who had founded it and had been the scene of a great battle at some point. According to the many history lessons he had tried his best not to listen to but had somehow made it into his brain anyway, Estrelle had the advantage of sitting in the valley between an ocean and a mountain range. Something about that made them harder to invade. Or was it easier? He couldn't remember.

A loud horn sounded from the town square below, and a few lulo birds emerged from the thick, colorful treetops.

"Hellooo to you, too, Chieftess Luna!" Engle yelled down to the village, waving. He could likely see her, even though they were still far away.

Tor sighed. His mother presided over all Eve festivities, wearing the traditional Emblemite clothing that he found slightly embarrassing. Still, he had to admit he was proud of her. She wanted to lead and was great at it, in part because of her emblem. It magnified traits that were already inside her, growing stronger with passion and practice. That was how it was for most Emblemites. Tor was surrounded by people who actually liked their markings. Rosa loved to sing, his father loved to cook. Engle loved to...stare?

Tor wasn't like them though, and he feared his mother would never understand. So he had taken matters into his own hands.

His father was in the kitchen when they arrived.

"Engle! Sapphire pie?" Anton Luna motioned toward a gooey, blue-spotted dessert that had just come out of the oven. When cooked at high enough temperatures, precious stones were sweeter than any other ingredient. Sapphire had a creamy, rich flavor.

"Two pieces," Engle said excitedly. "Actually, make it three." He had the biggest appetite Tor had ever seen—and not only for his father's delicious cooking.

Tor's father offered him a piece, too. "No thanks," he said, his stomach already full of nerves. By this time tomorrow, he could be free of his emblem. Even better, he could have a *new* one. The one he had always wanted.

Mr. Luna took a look at the clock, then slapped his hands together. "Festivities start in just a few, you two. Be sure to be ready."

Engle leapt off the bar stool he had settled on, already having inhaled his three pieces of pie. "Better get on home then." His eyes lit with anticipation. "I have to grab my wish." They said goodbye, knowing full well that he would be back in just a few minutes.

Rosa walked in from the living room. Her mouth was twisted into a sour pout. "Why am I too young to wish?"

Their father grinned and crouched so he was her size.

"Because if eight-year-olds' dreams came true, we'd have cake for breakfast each day, and school would be replaced by firefly hunting."

Rosa blinked. "That sounds amazing!"

Tor laughed. "What could you possibly have to wish for?" The minimum age limit for wishing was twelve—this was Tor's first time participating.

Rosa held her nose up high. "I want to be a sightseer like Engle!"

Tor raised an eyebrow. "I thought you loved singing."

"I do. I want to be a singer *and* a sightseer."

His father stopped smiling. "Rosa," he said, his voice stern. "You know the rules. We have *one* emblem, and one only. Anything more is too much."

"But—"

"End of discussion." He sighed, then patted her on the head. "Go get ready now, the both of you. We have a long night ahead of us."

Tor retreated to his room, closing the door behind him and standing with his back against it, for good measure. He felt as though there was a sea urchin lodged in his throat. Maybe *he* should be grateful for the emblem he had. Maybe he should forget his wish altogether.

He stood a little taller. No, he had waited too long. This

wasn't a rash decision; he had hated his mark for years, ever since he learned it would keep him from doing what he loved. Now he finally had a chance to do something about it.

When Tor was sure Rosa and his father were not going to barge in, he unearthed the leaf from his pocket and carefully unfolded it. To his relief, his wish was still visible, black ink against the vibrant green. Once an evergreen plant was written upon, it stayed fresh forever. He read the words out loud, in a whisper:

Instead of a leader, I wish to be a water-breather.

Rhyming wasn't a rule, but Tor hoped his attempt at one would improve the chances of his wish being granted. Maybe the mysterious wish-gods liked poetry? It couldn't hurt, he reasoned.

He knew it was time to leave the house when he heard the drummers—marching outside, their beats like bouts of thunder. Rosa opened the front door, and Tor watched the procession pass by, the sea of people resembling a current running through the streets. As soon as the singers came into view, Rosa readied herself, then jumped seamlessly into their group, her recognizable voice, high in pitch and sweet in melody, immediately braiding itself into the song.

Then it was Tor's turn to join the madness.

His senses were all flooded at the same time. Into his

ears, the music roared, plucks from a harp interrupted by beats of a drum, then put to rest by the echo of a horn being blown just ahead. Into his nose, the deep scents of fresh lavender-flavored croissants and flower-stuffed empanadas. Into his eyes, every color, a rainbow of leaves falling from the canopy of trees watching over the houses, orange baskets lifted high above heads, carrying lilac berries and golden apples. Onto his skin, the arms of fellow villagers pressed as they raced past him into the beautiful mess. Engle joined him on his right as the bonfire came into view.

His mother stood in front of it, in a headpiece made of a hundred feathers and flowers. Long ago everyone wore headpieces to the Eve celebration—and a few older villagers still did. Chieftess Luna's own had been passed on for generations, made using plumes from birds that no longer roamed the skies. Red-haired ravens, blue-tipped vultures. And, the object of many a magical tale, a single silver falcon feather.

The villagers wrapped around the fire. Tor stood so close that its warm, thick breath stung his cheeks. As the last person found their place, the crowd fell silent.

"Happy Eve," Chieftess Luna said, her words booming almost as loudly as her horn had. One of the advantages of being born a leader was having an exceptionally loud voice. Tor had one, too. But a gift was useless if it was never used.

"We celebrate the passing into a new year, into a new chapter of our lives. The wish-gods watch over us now, as they have for a thousand years, listening to our pleas and purest desires. Tonight, they reward the best of us, showing their strength and generosity to those that deserve it."

Tor swallowed. How could he have been so foolish? Of course his wish wouldn't be granted. If he was honest with himself, Tor knew he was probably the *least* deserving person standing there.

But...

Maybe the wish-gods would see he was only acting out because he had been gifted the entirely wrong marking. If anything, Tor might be the *exact* type of person they wanted to reward.

Yes, that sounded right. He had been living with the wrong emblem for years, of course he deserved to have his wish granted.

Hope bloomed in his chest once more.

Chieftess Luna continued, "This new year, may we be bolder, better, truer than we were before. May we fight for love, and love the fight. May we protect ourselves, and protect our rights. May we always stand as Emblemites. And for as long as the sky and sea run blue, may your wildest dreams have the chance to come true. For wishing is the bravest form of dreaming."

The village roared like a tidal wave, clapping and singing in approval. Even the fire grew just a little.

"Fetch the wishes." There was a rustling as the villagers reached into their pockets. Tor already had his in hand, squeezed so tightly he risked tearing it in half.

Chieftess Luna smiled. It was almost time. His heart felt like a balloon ready to burst. In a few moments, his entire life could be changed—a new fate could be set in motion.

"Now set them free."

Hundreds of wishes flew at the same second, an avalanche of leaves that turned the night air green. Tor watched his own leaf being eaten up, the corners crumbling, center burning, until it was gone. When the last wish was offered, the flames turned from copper to silver, for just a moment. Then, the fire disappeared altogether, leaving just a pile of purple ash.

Tor stood fixed in place as his fellow villagers made their way to the carts of food that lined the town square. Now that he had been freed of his wish, he felt somewhat lighter—but still full of enough anxiety to make his stomach lurch.

What would happen if his wish was not granted? He would surely have to continue his studies, continue to be molded by Mrs. Alma into the perfect future Chief... Maybe he would even have to finally follow his parents' orders and stop swimming.

No. He swallowed past the rising lump in his throat.

If his wish was to come true, he could not let those dark thoughts brew.

"This food is lightning." Engle was holding three different flavors of spun sugar, a bag of pop-pop, and a large glass of creamed tea. The air was electric. It was Eve, after all, the night Emblemites had waited an entire year for—the feast to end all feasts. Farmers peeled golden apples at lightning speed to feed demand, and children reached hungrily toward the giant red ruby cake Tor's father had spent days baking. The only thing Engle needed, Tor thought, was at least three more hands to hold more food.

"You're going to make yourself sick," he said, watching Engle finish his entire drink in a single gulp, then toss the cup in a trash barrel.

Engle proudly rubbed his middle. "This stomach's a fighter," he said. "Has served me well for a dozen years. I don't plan on it failing me tonight."

Tor shrugged.

Instead of worrying about what would happen if his wish didn't come true, he now considered what would happen if it *did*. He hadn't told his parents about wanting to be rid of his leadership emblem, let alone the fact that he wanted to be a water-breather instead. Now that seemed like a mistake. He had gone behind their backs.

Selfish. The word bubbled up in his throat, ready to be spoken aloud. He was so selfish. For months, he had only thought about how much he had wanted his wish. He should have considered someone other than himself.

But he deserved to be happy. And if his parents truly loved him, they would understand that.

Tor blinked as someone snapped their fingers in front of his nose.

"Are you in or not?" Engle asked.

"In for what?"

"Sneaking your mom's copy of *Cuentos.* It has the vanor story, doesn't it?" *The Book of Cuentos* was a collection of stories they had grown up reading as children, myths of curses and creatures.

But the tales they knew were watered-down, simplified. The worst parts taken out. The true tales were dark and deadly...the stuff of nightmares. His mother's book held the true stories.

Of course Tor was in.

The Cave of Cosas

O nce upon a boiling cauldron, there was a cave. The Cave of Cosas was not to be entered—though there was no door keeping anyone out. Cielo's mother had warned him to never even walk in its shadow.

It's cursed. Every piece of it.

Cielo listened. For a while. But then summer came, and he spent his afternoons in the fields around the cave, where the grass was so long it brushed his sides as he moved through it, running his hand along its top, like petting the back of a giant beast.

One night, Cielo fell asleep in it. When he awoke, the moon was a pearl above him, and stars blinked hello.

And there was something else.

A voice.

No—a whisper.

Cielo...

He sat up, toward the sound.

Toward the cave.

Is someone there? he asked into the darkness.

There was a moment of silence. Then, *come closer.*

Cielo swallowed. Wondered if he should turn around. He could see the twinkling of candles from his village at the edge of the field. Could even see his home, if he squinted.

I have something for you.

The voice sounded sweet as milk and honey. Kind, velvety.

He took a step forward.

Just a little closer...

And Cielo kept walking, until he was at the mouth of the cave.

There was a woman, bathed in light, standing just inside. She wore flowing fabrics that changed color before his eyes. And there was a chest.

It swung open to reveal gems sparkling through the night, like stars plucked from the galaxy.

That's for me? he asked, eyes wide. Focused on the jewels. He had never wanted anything more in his life.

You can keep whatever you can fit in your pockets, the woman said.

He took a step forward, hands already wide open, fingers curved.

But the moment he entered the cave, the woman vanished. The gems turned to dust in his palms.

Cielo stumbled backward, then gasped. The field had shriveled up, grass to dirt, crops to rocks. *No, no...*

He screamed out as the emblem on his wrist scabbed over and fell away—and something else formed in its place. An eye, with an iris dark as night.

A curse.

And no one ever entered the Cave of Cosas again.

3

CURSED

Tor woke up to a new year without the help of the sun shining through his window or the smell of his father's January cakes, a stack of violet pancakes that guaranteed the family would start off the year on a sweet note. He stretched. He felt fine. Refreshed. It was a good morning.

Then, with a jolt, he remembered his wish.

A confetti of nerves burst in his chest. His arms were covered by pajamas. All he had to do was peel back his sleeve...

He did, and gasped. His emblem...

It was gone. And something sat in its place.

"Oh no," Tor said, rubbing at his wrist. "No, no, no, no." This could not be happening.

There was the symbol of an eye where the purple rings used to be, a marking crafted out of a dark, swirling ink. Just as he rubbed at it again, the new emblem did the unthinkable.

It *blinked*.

Tor barely managed to muffle a scream. He had read about this kind of marking just last night in *The Book of Cuentos*. His wish had clearly upset the wish-gods.

And he had been cursed for it.

Someone knocked on his door. He rushed to pull his sleeve down. "Come in," he said, voice cracking.

Chieftess Luna poked her head inside, smiling. "How was your Eve? I heard you ran out a little early." Tor gritted his teeth. Sometimes it felt like his mother had the entire village spying on him. It really was a wonder she still didn't know about his swimming sessions.

A lie snaked down his tongue, ready to be spoken, but he swallowed it down. Sneaking out of last night's festivities was the *least* of his worries. "Engle and I went looking for your copy of *Cuentos*," he admitted.

"Ah." She sat down at the foot of his bed. "I will assume I've kept it well hidden?"

He nodded sheepishly. Engle and Tor had searched all over. They'd ended up reading "The Cave of Cosas" for the hundredth time from Engle's parents' copy, which was missing most of its pages.

The Chieftess laughed, her head bobbing back. "If I can't protect my own son from that frightening book, how am I supposed to protect a village?" She smiled at him. "Not to worry, you'll study them at some point. The future chief of Estrelle needs to know the island's tales."

Future chief.

Tor's stomach lurched.

He didn't *have* his leadership bands anymore; he was no longer eligible to be his mother's successor. The thought brought him a crumb of relief, but mostly an unexpected tsunami of shame.

When she found out, she would be so disappointed.

"Is everything okay?" his mom asked.

"Everything's great," he said. He didn't want to lie, but what choice did he have? "I just want this new year to go smoothly."

His mother's eyes softened. "It will," she said encouragingly. "Your lifeline says so. You're to have a nice, comfortable life."

Tor almost wanted to laugh—or possibly cry.

If he was destined to have a boring life, how could he have been cursed? Was his wish truly so terrible?

She stood. "Your father is at the restaurant early, and I'm off to the office." She always had an early morning meeting

35

the day after Eve, to discuss how the event had gone. "January cakes are on the table." He received one last encouraging smile before she left. A few moments later, the front door closed. Rosa had already left for chorus, so Tor was alone.

He paced around his room, then around the kitchen, then around the family's dinner table. As if walking in large circles was a dance that could fix all of his problems.

No, no, no, no. Even if curses had at some point in time been real, they should have died out, like trolls and gnomes. They should have been a thing of the past, like the plague...or strange haircuts. Right?

He lifted his sleeve just a little. The eye stared back at him.

No, this curse was very real.

The front door flew open, and Tor jumped about two feet into the air. It was Engle, holding his stomach. "Staying home from school today," he mumbled, his expression pained. "Think I ate a little bit too much last night. Do you have miel tea?"

Under normal circumstances, Tor might have said something to the effect of *I told you so.* But today, his eyes widened and heart dropped as Engle's own all-seeing eyes found his wrist.

His friend's pained expression quickly shifted into one of disbelief. "*No*," he said, eyebrows nearly to his hairline.

Tor sighed. "Yes."

Engle ran Mr. Luna's cooking rag in hot water and wiped it roughly against Tor's skin, like the eye was ink that could be rubbed away with enough effort. When that didn't work, he tried using his palm for good measure. After a few minutes, the eye blinked, then squinted, glaring right at them. Engle stumbled backward.

"Yeah, that's not coming off," he said matter-of-factly.

"What's not coming off?"

Tor gasped, while Engle whipped around to face the front door.

"What are you doing here?" Tor asked.

"And how do you keep sneaking up on us?" Engle said, stepping to the side to shield Tor and his new mark. "Surprised she doesn't have an invisibility emblem," he murmured.

Melda crossed her arms. "It's twenty minutes into class. I told Mrs. Alma I would get you." She sighed. "You really should be thanking me. Before I offered to come here, she was talking about sending word to your mother."

Tor put his hands together behind his back. "Well, I'm not feeling well, so if you could go back and tell Mrs. Alma, that would be great."

Melda glared at him. "Not so fast." She walked past Engle until she was standing right in front of Tor. She placed her hands on her hips. "Hiding something?"

ALEX ASTER

Tor backed toward the kitchen. "Don't know what you're talking about."

She frowned, then examined her nails with a studied casualness. "You know, I could probably help." There she was again, Tor thought, always trying to solve everybody else's problems.

Engle snorted. "You?"

Melda squinted her eyes so much they resembled coin slots. "Yes, me. *That*," she pointed toward Tor's arm, "looks like a curse. And I happen to know of someone on Emblem Island who might be able to help you."

Tor flinched, wondering how Melda had gotten a look at the eye. He needed to be more careful. If word spread that he had been cursed, his reputation in town would be finished. He would have to leave Estrelle. He might even be sent to one of the more intense, stricter schools in the east. One miles away from any ocean...

Not only that, but what would happen to his parents? Would his mother have to step down as Chieftess?

Engle tilted his head to the side. "And where might that person live?"

She grinned, twirling one of the many blue ribbons in her hair between her fingers. "I'm not saying unless I get to come."

Engle opened his mouth, undoubtedly about to say something like *absolutely not*, when Tor cut him off.

"Fine," he said, making Engle sigh. He didn't have time to play games. If Melda really knew someone who could help him remove the curse, he needed to find them, and preferably before dinner. He packed all the money he had into his backpack, in case this person wanted payment.

Tor turned to Melda, who wore a pleased look on her pointed, heart-shaped face, and wondered if he would regret his next few words.

"Lead the way."

4

THE HERMIT'S HUT

Melda wouldn't say a word about where she was taking Tor and Engle. The corners of her lips turned up deviously, as if she took great pleasure in knowing something they didn't. Of course she did, Tor thought. This was *Melda*, after all, the same girl who for the past six years had taken any opportunity to make herself look better than him in class.

"If you won't tell us where, at least tell us *who*," Engle said as they stepped into the forest. They had used the house's back door, leading directly into the woods. The last thing Tor wanted was to be spotted by Mrs. Guava, the nosy, porch-knitting neighbor who lived one tree over.

"Well, she's a bit of a hoarder," Melda said, squinting at the sky, looking like she was trying to find another word to describe the woman. "A *collector*, if you want to put it nicely."

Engle scrunched his nose. "And what exactly does she collect?"

"Information. She knows everything about everything."

Tor stopped dead in his tracks. "She's a know-all?" The owl-shaped emblem of a know-all was one of the rarest marks gifted.

"We haven't had one of those near Estrelle for years, as far as I know," Engle said. Tor nodded in agreement. He looked to Melda.

She shrugged. "She's a bit of a hermit. Doesn't get out much. And she *is* a know-all."

Tor straightened. He never thought he would meet one in the flesh. They tended to reside in big cities, as advisers to the leaders there. "How did you find her?"

She grinned widely and Tor sighed, preparing himself for a long story. He guessed she wasn't used to having an audience. "Well, I was looking for a source for a paper last year. The one about significant political events in the last century?" She glanced at Tor, and he nodded, even though he had no idea what she was talking about. Probably because he hadn't written that paper. "Well, I was writing *mine* on the great droughts of Tortuga Bay, and how it was impacting their economy—they live mostly on oysters you know, and—"

Engle groaned. "The short version, please."

Melda's mouth formed a tight line. "I had one of the students with a tracking emblem help me locate a book I needed, one that had been checked out of the library for twenty years. Turns out, the know-all had it." She crossed her arms in front of her.

"See, that wasn't too hard, was it?" Engle said.

She shot him a glare in response.

Tor snuck a look at his wrist. Some part of him hoped the eye would simply have disappeared...and that they could all go to school.

School. He almost wanted to laugh. He had never wanted to sit in Mrs. Alma's class more in his life.

He gulped when he found that the eye still sat on his wrist, opened wide. Taunting him.

Melda pressed a finger against it, making Tor rip his arm away.

"Don't do that," he yelled. The eye blinked a few times, angry.

"Sorry," she said, looking at her fingertip as if to see if it had left a mark.

They walked the rest of the way in silence, Engle kicking up dirt with each step. After a couple of thunderous stomach growls, he groaned. "How far is this place? I'm starving." He seemed to have recovered from his stomachache rather quickly. He sniffed the air like a dog that had just caught a whiff of dinner. "Do you smell that?"

Tor did smell that. There was something distinctly sweet in the breeze, reminding him of a cinnamon roll or one of those lavender-icing-covered donuts his father made when Rosa had a concert. Before he could stop him, Engle was off, following the smell like it would lead him to a mound of treasure.

"Wait!" Melda yelled, falling far behind. She said a few other things, too, but Tor couldn't make out the words as he rushed to catch up.

A few more trees and a close encounter with a low branch later, Tor found Engle in front of a hut. It was built out of branches and leaves, blending in with the surrounding woods. Vines crept in and out of the windows, tying themselves all around the base, like the house had been taken hostage by the forest.

Melda skidded to a stop behind them, huffing and puffing as though she had run a much farther distance than they had. She was trying to say something, but through all of the heavy breathing and wheezing, Tor couldn't understand a word of it.

They all cried out at the same time. A cat as tall as two of them put together and covered in what looked like spikes careened through a window and blocked their path.

The front door flew open, and a small, rounded woman

stuck her red face out. "Back, Whiskers!" she yelled. The cat froze, just a foot away from the trio. Tor swore he could hear his own heart beating. A moment later, the creature's eyes closed, and its spikes—which Tor now recognized as raised fur—began to settle down, making it look half as large. It was made of mostly hair.

"That's a barbed malkin," Engle whispered, voice trembling in a mixture of awe and fear.

Once the animal crept back inside the hut, fitting through an impossibly small sliver in an open door, the woman frowned. "And what do you want?" she asked.

Melda stepped forward. "Um, hello, Mrs. Libra. Lovely... *pet* you have there. Do you remember me?"

The woman's expression did not change. "Whiskers isn't a pet, he's a messenger." Then, her tiny chia seed eyes squinted. "And of course I remember you. How could I forget the little girl that ruined my ten-year streak as a successful hermit?"

Melda laughed nervously and shoved a hand in one of her pockets. Tor wondered how Melda could afford the blue lace that trimmed her pockets.

"Sorry to disturb you—er—again. But we could really use your help."

The woman shook her head, then started to close the door. That was when Melda pushed Tor forward.

"Show her!" she yelled.

Tor held up his arm and yanked on his sleeve.

Mrs. Libra blinked, and the cursed eye blinked back. The woman's face paled. "Come in," she said, holding the door open again. "Quickly."

The moment Tor stepped inside the hut, he realized Melda's description of Mrs. Libra as a hoarder had been a gross understatement. Towers of books reached from floor to ceiling on almost every inch of the floor and wobbled back and forth when Mrs. Libra slammed the door shut. It was a wonder they didn't all topple over or knock into each other like giant dominoes.

"Careful," Mrs. Libra said, expertly navigating a narrow trail that created a sort of maze through the columns of books. She carved a path through the mess like an underground mole. "One of these falls over, and it'll bury you. That's how Mr. Libra passed, bless his heart."

Engle shot Tor a horrified look.

The next room was not nearly as organized as the first. It held mounds of mess—a pile of pots and pans taller than Tor, an endless sea of ripped-out pages, bookcases and chairs that had been stacked one on top of the other, as if to make wood for a giant bonfire.

Tor exhaled in relief when they moved out of that room

and into the next. That was, until he hit his head against a rather large text. He rubbed his forehead and blinked a few times in disbelief.

Dozens of books hung from the ceiling by pieces of string, creating some sort of floating library. They swayed back and forth, and Tor was reminded of the giant holiday ornaments that had, up until recently, decorated the town tree. Mrs. Libra seemed to have her own organizational system, because she walked right up to a book hanging in one corner of the room and opened it up.

Her finger jabbed a page that had a drawing of the exact mark Tor had sprouted on his wrist, an eye with veiny spiderwebs for lashes. "It's a witch's curse. Knew it the second I saw it," Mrs. Libra said.

"*Witch's* curse?" Tor said in disbelief. Witch was a foul name for a person who had been born with multiple emblems. Possessing more than one was considered strange. Evil, in some circles. Too much power to be held responsibly. History had taught the Emblemites that a person with that much ability would always be driven to do dark deeds.

This was taking it too far. First curses, now talk of a witch? As far as Tor knew, there hadn't been an active one in years.

Mrs. Libra gave him a look. "That's what I said."

"There *are* no witches."

She smirked. "I didn't say *witches,* plural, I said *witch.* The Night Witch."

Tor blinked. There was a moment of quiet. Then, he barked out a laugh. "The *Night Witch*?" He turned to Engle, who snorted. Melda was the only one who looked grim. But, then again, that was how she always looked. "That's a fairy tale! *Cuentos* stuff."

The hermit's face turned a remarkable shade of red, anger building in her face like boiling water. She turned sharply on her heel and yanked a book clean off its string. Tor recognized it immediately, with its black cover and delicate, silver title.

The Book of Cuentos.

And not the one he had in his room. This one looked exactly like his mother's. Raw, completely unedited. Every story intact.

She turned to the last chapter, thumbing the pages so hard she risked tearing a hole right through them. When she found the right illustration, she turned the book to face Tor, the parchment just an inch from his nose.

He knew the drawing before his eyes had a chance to focus—the outline of a woman with dark hair and coals for eyes.

The Night Witch. The queen of Emblem Island nightmares, the overly used threat against children, the protagonist of often-murmured superstitions.

Don't wear a braid to bed, or the Night Witch will cut it off in your sleep.

Bad luck from the Night Witch travels in threes.

Keep an upside-down broom behind the door to keep the Night Witch from sneaking inside.

But those were pieces of foolish folklore—they never came true. The Lunas had never once put a broom behind the door, and, as far as he knew, the Night Witch had never paid them a visit.

The hermit closed the book hard, a cloud of dust erupting from its pages. "Have more respect for your island's history, boy," she said stormily, before pressing the book to his chest. "Best read up."

History? Tor couldn't believe he was even entertaining the thought that any of those stories were true. But the proof of their reality was embedded right into his skin. "If she's real, then how do I make this Night Witch's curse go away?"

The hermit scrunched her eyebrows together, and dozens of vertical wrinkles formed between them. With her round body, reddish face, and crinkles, Tor thought she looked very much like an overripe plum. "Well, isn't it obvious?" She threw her arms up in exasperation. "You have to find the witch."

Tor almost choked on his own tongue. "What?"

48

That was a task he certainly could not complete before dinner. Engle's stomach growled behind him.

"Yes, and best hurry," she said, taking Tor's hand into her own and placing a sharp nail against his palm. She tapped against his lifeline, and Tor gasped.

His lifeline had been changed—cut short. He had been so busy staring at his curse that he hadn't even noticed.

Tor's long, boringly flat line was gone. A short one scattered with valleys sat in its place...

And it ended in a sharp drop.

Tor knew what that meant, and so did Melda, who steadied herself by grabbing one of the hanging books.

By the looks of it, Tor was very close to the end of his life.

The hermit nodded solemnly. "I would say you have about a week. Give or take."

"How do you know?" Engle asked, breathless.

She gave him a look.

"Where is the Night Witch?" Tor sputtered, suddenly a believer. "Where do I find her?" If anyone knew, it had to be the know-all. According to the last story in *Cuentos*, the Night Witch lived in a castle on a cliff. But that could be anywhere on Emblem Island.

Mrs. Libra shuffled a few feet away, and murmured, "I have a map here somewhere..." She looked over her shoulder at them. "Ah—forgot to mention. Don't let anyone touch that dark emblem. That's about the *last* thing you'd want to do."

Melda and Engle shared a wide-eyed look. "What happens to people who touch the marking?" she asked, her voice in a ridiculous high pitch.

Mrs. Libra smirked, and Tor pressed his teeth together to keep a sudden flash of annoyance at bay. That was the thing with know-alls. From what he had heard, their know-allness toward people who did *not* know everything made them pretty unlikable. Tor wondered if Mrs. Libra was a hermit by choice or simply didn't have any friends. "The curse latches on to their body, too, of course. Practically *everyone* knows that."

Melda gasped, while Engle cried out. They hurried to push their sleeves back.

"I've got an eye!" Melda screamed. It blinked hello.

"I have its mouth!" Tor and Melda turned to see a pair of lips on Engle's wrist. They smiled deviously.

But it was worse than that. Just like Tor, both Engle and Melda's lifelines had been cut short.

"That's hogwash!" Engle said. "I had a pretty deep valley coming up." He crossed his arms across his chest in disappointment. "Wanted to find out what it was going to be."

Melda laughed without humor. "Well, I'd say *this* qualifies."

She turned to face Tor. He noticed she still had her leadership bands, and Engle still had his telescope marking. Since they hadn't made the forbidden wish, it seemed the curse had only affected their lifelines. That, at least, was a relief. "This is your fault," she said, poking an accusatory finger at him.

She ran her other hand through her black hair, then stomped her foot with enough force to knock a pile of something over in the next room. "What was your stupid wish anyway?"

Tor dropped his gaze to the dirt-coated floor. He didn't want to say. In his mind, the truth sounded foolish enough, and he suspected saying it aloud would make it seem even worse.

He could lie instead, say he had wished for Emblem Island–wide peace, or a new, more reliable well for the village...

As tempting as that was, Tor knew Melda deserved the true answer. Especially now that she shared his curse. He sighed. "I wished to be rid of my leadership emblem."

Melda gaped at him, as shocked as if he had confessed to wishing for a hurricane. "Why would you ever do that?" she asked, horrified. Tor immediately regretted being so honest. Of course *she* wouldn't understand. Just like his mother, she practically worshipped the purple bands around her wrist.

He gritted his teeth. "Because I don't want to be a chief.

I don't want to lead." The part of the answer he kept from her was: *I want to be something else.*

Melda's face looked frozen, as if she'd stepped right into an arctic pond and floated up stuck inside a glacier. Finally, she began to thaw, her mouth closing and eyebrows coming down. The look she gave him next was a surprise...

She almost seemed disappointed.

Tor had expected her to be at least a little excited. If her one-upping in class was any indication, Melda would have given all of her precious ribbons to be Estrelle's future Chieftess. The fact Tor's mother was the current town leader meant he was the first choice to follow in her footsteps, but *now*, perhaps Melda's future held something greater than simply being elected to the village's council.

Tor grimaced, reality setting in. No, right about now, her future was an untimely death at the hands of a curse.

And it was all his fault.

"Well, this is marvelous," Melda growled, looking up at the dust-caked ceiling. "I know *you two*," she shot a pointed look at Engle and Tor, "probably spend your time playing on those death-trap twinetrees, or reading *Cuentos*, or tracking animals, or any number of ridiculous activities, but I have *responsibilities*." Tor was surprised to see tears in her eyes. She turned toward the wall, sniffled, and wiped at something on her face before turning back around again. "I have people who need me."

Tor wanted to counter that he had people who needed him, too—like Rosa, and maybe even his parents. But he knew Melda's situation was different.

Engle shrugged. "No one will even notice I left."

"I just don't know how my mom will manage," Melda said in a small voice. With a rocky breath, she faced Mrs. Libra, who had been pretending to leaf through a book, but whose ears had been pointed toward their conversation. "We're going to be needing that map."

Having come to the agreement that the three of them would not be making it back to school that day—or dinner, much to Engle's displeasure—they enlisted Mrs. Libra's cat to leave a note on Tor's front door. They attached the paper to its back and hoped for the best.

OFF ON AN ADVENTURE. BE BACK SOON-ISH.

TOR, ENGLE, AND MELDA

Once the feline had gone on its way, Mrs. Libra fetched the map. She took a rusty pin out of her mosslike hair and used it to tack the top of the parchment to the wall. The rest unrolled almost all the way to the floor.

Tor sucked in a deep breath of the hut's sweet and sour scents. Sure, he had studied maps in his leadership classes before. Dozens, even. Part of a leader's role was being familiar with one's territory. Still, they had only studied local maps of Estrelle and its surrounding settlements. Beyond that, he only vaguely knew what the rest of Emblem Island looked like. Not many people in his village had traveled farther than the mountain ranges, and those who had told stories too wild to believe.

"Where on here is the witch's castle?" Engle asked, eyes moving back and forth at lightning speed.

Mrs. Libra shrugged. "I don't know."

Melda blinked several times. "You...you *don't know*?" One eye twitched, and she looked about ready to strangle something. "Aren't you a know-all?"

"Why, yes. Of course I am."

"So—and *please do* correct me if your title is vastly misleading—but aren't you supposed to, you know..." She closed her fists. "Know it *all*?"

"Know-alls have geographical limits," Mrs. Libra

scoffed. "I know everything about this village, all the way to the edge of the forest. Outside of that is beyond my jurisdiction."

Melda slapped her own forehead in a way that looked like it might have hurt. "Geographical limits?" she repeated.

"That's what I said, please do pay attention."

Tor spoke before Melda could say something they might *all* regret. "So, what *can* you tell us?"

The hermit pointed at the map. "The next know-all lives in the city of Zeal. Works as the queen's adviser. Go there, and he'll have more information for you."

Engle snorted. "And just how do you suppose we manage that? I've been to Zeal, and you need a balloon ticket to get there." He was right. The only way to get past the thick ring of mountains that surrounded the village was by holding one of the giant, vibrant balloons that were enchanted to land on the other side. Tor knew even if they did manage to get tickets, going over the mountains was not an option. The sightseer who guarded the perimeter of Estrelle would spot them right away—and alert their parents.

Mrs. Libra tapped the map, directing their attention to a long passageway Tor hadn't noticed. "That's where you're wrong. A tunnel runs just beneath the mountain ring." The know-all squinted, staring at the blue necklace Melda always wore. "Is that—" Melda put the pendant back inside her shirt before Mrs. Libra could finish her sentence.

Tor focused on the passageway beneath the mountains. "If there's a tunnel, why do so many people use the balloons?"

The hermit pursed her thin lips, wrinkles sprouting out of her mouth like tree roots. "I suppose some people...though I can't imagine who...find that specific mode of transportation...*fun*." She said the last word with the disgust of someone talking about finding an insect in their food. "The real reason villagers don't take the tunnel, of course, is that it's not the safest of passages."

What could be worse than holding on to a balloon string for dear life? Tor wondered. It was as if the know-all read his mind.

"Not well lit, for starters. How did they phrase it in that book?" She walked over to another corner, mumbling to herself, before spotting the right text and throwing it open. The hermit clicked her tongue until she found the right page. "Ah, yes, here it is. The tunnel is described as being in *complete and total, absolute darkness.*"

Melda and Tor turned to face Engle, whose sightseeing emblem gave him the ability to see not only long distances, but also in the dark. He shrugged. "I can get us through. But to do that, I'm going to need something."

Mrs. Libra nodded. "Of course. I have a map of the tunnels somewhere..."

Engle blinked. "Oh." He rubbed his stomach. "That's good, but I was talking about the peppermint rolls I've been smelling since we got here."

They left the hermit's hut with a sack full of peppermint rolls and two maps. Mrs. Libra's expression sunk back into a cavernous frown. "Never come again," she said before slamming the door in Tor's face.

Engle licked each of his fingers, having eaten three rolls already. "These are almost better than your dad's, Tor," he said. "No offense to him, of course. Or to you." He looked pensive. "Or to your dad's rolls..." Just a few yards into the forest, he stopped and gave Tor a serious look. "Should we turn around and get more?"

Melda sighed. "Only if you plan on eating all of them before anyone else can take a bite. There are *three* of us on this journey, you know."

Engle ignored her and talked around another pastry. "Say, Melda, you have four brothers, right?"

"*Five*," she said haughtily. "They're quintuplets."

He continued to chew with his mouth open. "They're always sick, right?" Tor shot Engle a look. "What?" he said. "That's what you told me."

Tor wanted to dig a hole and climb into it.

Melda gave them both a mean look. "Not that it's any of your business, but yes, they are *always sick*. They have howling cough." Tor winced. Howling cough was a particularly vile sickness that resulted in constant, high-pitched coughing. "Now, if you're done with your questions, I would appreciate some silence." She looked down at the map, clearly dismissing them both.

Though Engle kept his mouth shut, the forest was far from silent. Rainbow-beaked toucans crooned, howling palm-sized chiquita monkeys shrieked, and orange-spotted toads croaked in their rich baritone. Rosa loved to venture into these same woods with Tor; she liked the music of it.

"We're getting close," Melda finally said, after almost an hour of walking. The sky had started to deepen into the darker blue of early afternoon, and the mountains loomed overhead, casting them in shade. A section of the roll of parchment was spread out in front of her face, her nose practically brushing the paint as she studied it carefully. Tor peered over her shoulder. According to the map, the entrance to the mountain's tunnels was just a few feet farther...

Melda managed to scream once before falling completely out of view.

The Night Witch

O nce upon a screaming white moon, a Night Witch was born.

As a child, she spoke to the willow trees, whispered to the garden bees, and had a smile so sweet it dripped golden honey. When she brushed her hair, starlight fell to the ground. When she passed by, flowers fell from her fingertips. And when she cried, it stormed.

So sweet she looked, her smile hid the darkness waiting behind it.

She had a gift never seen before. The power to kill with a single touch.

And kill she did.

One day, the girl emerged from her home, covered in blood, her father's emblem on her skin. She walked through the village, barefoot, and never looked back. She traveled across the island, leaving only death in her wake, emblems appearing on her arms after each kill, the ones she had stolen from children in their beds and from the poor souls who found themselves alone on a dark night.

Hungry for more power, the girl spread curses like plagues, ones that poisoned rivers and fields full of crops, each new death adding to her collection of abilities.

Thus, the moonlit girl became the dark-haired witch.

Now, when she brushes her hair, ash falls to the ground. When she passes by, blood falls from her fingers. And each time she cries, a star falls from the sky.

5

THE TROLL TUNNELS

Tor and Engle stared down into a dark, dark hole. The opening had been covered by a bush that Melda had taken down with her. Tor hoped very much that its leaves had somehow cushioned her fall.

Engle squinted. "She's all right," he said, seeing something Tor could not. "It's not as deep as it looks, just dark."

"Is it the tunnel?"

Engle nodded. "Looks like it."

Tor motioned forward with his chin. Even though Engle said Melda was okay, that didn't mean he was ready to throw himself into the darkness. Or, at least, not until his friend did. "Go on, then."

Engle shrugged, then jumped right into the hole, eliciting

a scream from below. Tor heard Melda's voice: "You landed right on my foot!"

"Did you not have the good sense to move?"

"Well, excuse me for thinking that someone with the gift of sightseeing would see my big toe!"

Tor sighed. "I'm coming down," he yelled, their fighting taking the fear right out of the jump. Then, he, too, joined them in the dark.

Even with the small hole of sunlight raining down, the tunnel was the closest to pitch black Tor had ever experienced. No color lived down there, just dirt stone walls, and musky air.

After a few moments of thick silence, Engle's voice rang through the passage. "Grab on to my arms, I'll lead you through." he said. They reached out and held on to him tightly, then walked forward blindly.

Tor heard a crinkling of paper and assumed Engle was unfurling the map. "All right. We take four right turns, then two lefts. We can remember that, right?" he asked.

"We better," Tor said. He repeated the directions in his mind again. If they made one wrong turn, they could be lost in the underground maze forever.

Satisfied, Engle tucked the parchment away, and they started their journey into the center of the mountain range.

Tor never thought he would find himself in a place like

this—below millions of pounds of rock, miles of land above him, underneath a ceiling that could cave in at any moment. He was meant to have a smooth, uneventful future. Children with featureless lifelines lived similar lives to Tor's grandfather, who spent his days tending to a small garden and had never left Estrelle. *A nice, comfortable life.*

Now, anything was possible...including an early death. A chill snaked down his spine.

Still, if Tor allowed himself to be the least bit optimistic, he knew the stripping of his lifeline meant he might just have a chance at changing his future. If he could find the Night Witch and convince her to rid him of his curse, Tor could create a new lifeline. One filled with more peaks than the Scalawag Range, just like Rosa.

But Tor wasn't sure he could convince the Night Witch of anything, even if they did manage to find her. He had read her story, more times than he could count.

Which meant he knew what he was up against.

They walked the next few miles in a silence only interrupted by Engle's stomach growls, which marked five-minute intervals with surprising accuracy. When they reached the first right turn, Tor exhaled in relief, hoping their trip in the dark would almost be over. But the tunnel stretched on.

It was not long before Engle began to sigh, clearly upset

that this was no time for snacking. Or perhaps he was bored. In any case, he started to complain about everything around him, from the mold-like smell, to the dust, to the tiny rocks that occasionally fell from the ceiling, raining down onto their heads like hail. When he was done grumbling about the tunnels, he quickly turned the attention of his laser-sharp eyes to another target.

"There's something in your hair, Melda."

She ignored him.

"It's moving."

"Let it move."

"It's glowing."

"Let it glow."

"It's—"

"Would you please stuff your mouth with a peppermint roll so that we don't have to hear your ridiculous squeaky voice anymore?"

That shut him up. And he very happily stuffed his mouth with a peppermint roll. Engle had been right, however. There was something in Melda's hair, shining ever so slightly.

It was a few moments later that Melda spoke again. "Um, boys?"

"Yes?" Tor said.

She swallowed. "This is going to sound severely stupid."

"Then best not embarrass yourself," Engle said.

There was a moment of silence, and Tor would have bet all of the dobbles in his backpack that Melda was glaring at Engle.

His friend sighed dramatically. "What is it?"

"Well." She cleared her throat. "I still can't really see anything, and it might just be my mind making things up, but, are the walls...are they *moving*?"

Tor expected Engle to snort, or make a rude comment, but instead he replied, in a very tiny voice, "Yes."

They came to a rough halt. That's when Tor noticed that with the faint light in Melda's hair he, too, could make out that the long cracks along the walls looked a bit like the outlines of creatures with curved noses and long, twisting tree-root fingers. He suddenly remembered a jingle about a mountain troll, something Rosa used to sing when she was little. He squinted, trying to remember the words. Was there something about a warning? Something about teeth?

Melda gasped.

Suddenly, there were not just cracks but also *eyes* in the walls, blinking open. They were alive with something Tor recognized immediately, given how long he had known Engle...

Hunger.

With screams that echoed in front of and behind them,

they broke into a run, barely able to see and with nowhere to go but forward. When they reached a fork in the road, Melda managed to remember to turn right, just as Tor risked a look over his shoulder.

"Faster!" Tor yelled as he watched the faint outline of a troll peeling itself from the wall and heading directly their way. Melda was gasping as if her lungs were on the verge of total collapse.

"They smell your stupid peppermint rolls!" she yelled, chest rising and falling like there was a rabid animal stuck behind her ribs. They made another right turn.

Engle made a face. "It's not the rolls making their mouths water."

The light in Melda's hair was brighter now, and Tor could see her blue eyes become the size of chestnuts.

The tunnel rang with growls and the sounds of dozens of large, pattering feet. And with so much echoing noise, it was impossible to know how close the beasts were.

Another right turn. Just two more lefts to go.

Engle gripped his friends' arms tightly. Tor could feel Engle's palms getting slippery with sweat.

Something like a small gust of wind tickled the back of Tor's neck...something like a breeze. *Impossible.* They were miles and miles underground.

But there it was again, a stream of air blowing his hair across his own sweat-stained forehead.

Tor had a feeling he would regret it, but he looked over his shoulder anyway, trusting that Engle and Melda could lead the way. Hot breath blasted across his face. With a growl, a troll reached forward, and Tor screamed as its claw ran down the length of his arm.

He tumbled, inhaling a cloud of pulverized rock. Dozens of jaws snapped at the air just above him, the trolls trying to get a mouthful of flesh.

Tor squeezed his eyes shut, afraid that even in the dark, he'd see death coming in the form of a troll's gaping mouth. He braced for the sensation of coral-sharp teeth sinking deep into his skin, and the warmth of his own blood puddling beneath him.

Tor heard a sound he thought likely to be his last: his friends' screams.

"Get away from him!"

"Take the peppermint rolls instead!"

A grunt, as one of them kicked at a troll.

"Leave!" Tor yelled, trying not to let the fear in his voice show. "Get out of here and save yourselves!"

He was half-disappointed and half-grateful when he realized they were not following his orders. He wasn't a leader anymore, after all.

"Tor!" Melda yelled. "Don't let them bite you, Engle says not to—"

He screamed.

It was like a giant needle had skewered his toes. Sparks of pain ignited in his bones. His entire foot went numb, and Tor was sure the troll had bitten it clean off.

A moment later, Melda screamed, too. "Ow, my hair!"

And all at once, there was light—a halo of it surrounding Engle's outstretched hand. A carrot-sized woman was wriggling in his grip, glowing from head to toe.

The trolls looked up from where they were crouched over Tor. One glance and they all let out a bloodcurdling shriek.

The mountain creatures turned, still screeching, trying to run away. But as soon as the bright light found their leathery skin, they hardened back into stone, one by one. Right where they stood, they froze—arms still outstretched, eyes still wide, and hungry mouths still open.

And then there was silence.

Melda ran to Tor's side and wrapped one of the many ribbons from her hair around the place the troll had scratched him.

Engle helped him to his feet, and Tor was happy to find he still had two. "Don't worry, troll bites are nothing but annoying," his friend said. "Their teeth release just a bit of a chemical that promotes drowsiness, making it hard for their victims to escape. You know, kind of like how the snaggletooth viper has venom that paralyzes its prey?" Tor had no idea what Engle was talking about, but felt suddenly grateful for his friend's fascination with deadly creatures.

Miles from the sun, it seemed the trolls' weakness was light—and Engle's quick thinking was likely the only reason Tor was still alive. He limped forward, foot dragging lamely behind him, most of his weight on Engle.

He looked down at his friend's palm. The fairy had turned back into a flower—their preferred state—but was still giving off a soft glow.

Melda sighed. "Must have gotten lodged in my hair when I fell through the bush," she explained.

Engle shrugged. "Well, I did tell you that you had something stuck in your—" He was cut short by an especially severe glare. He pushed the flower back into Melda's hair, and there it stayed, acting as both their protection and guiding light as they made their way out of the troll tunnels.

THE HYDROCLOPS

O nce upon a scarlet heart, a man fell in love with a woman and gifted her his most prized possession—a forever-blooming flower. One he promised would never die, just like their love.

But promises, like snowflakes, are easily broken. Just a few springs into their marriage, the lovely wife learned that her husband had fallen for another maiden, with cheeks that bloomed red as dawn.

Consumed by grief and jealousy, she climbed the highest mountain peak she could find, and yelled a single wish to the heavens divine: *make it be that my husband can never leave me.*

And so, her wish was granted.

The next morning, upon awakening, the woman found she had no arms to stretch above her head, no fingers to brush away the hair that had always fallen onto her cheeks. In fact, she had no hair left at all. The wife blinked, and found she had but one, giant eye. She opened her mouth to scream, but discovered she could only hiss...

She was forever bound to her husband, both turned into serpents, connected. One head on each end.

Tied together for eternity.

And so, the first hydroclops was created.

6

THE CITY OF ZEAL

As soon as they were out of the caves, the fairy flew away, taking a chunk of Melda's black hair with it. "Ow!" she yelled, rubbing her scalp. They had exited through a small opening at the base of the mountain, so tiny they had to slide on their stomachs to get out. Tor found that his foot was almost all the way mobile again, except for a few of his toes. Engle was right about the venom's drowsiness effects. Tor felt as though he could sleep the rest of his lifeline away.

They laid down for a few minutes in silence, staring up at the sun that looked so much more useful than it had before. The city stood high in the distance, only a flat plain between them.

Engle started to snore, and Melda kicked him. "We're not taking a nap," she said, getting up. "Come on, then. We'll want to find the know-all before nightfall."

The City of Zeal was an artificially colorful place. Unlike their village, which boasted trees with leaves of every hue, a sea the bluest of blue, and animals with multicolored fur, this city was natureless—built entirely of stone and made up of people who wore dyed clothing and jewelry cut from precious gems.

It was a place of decadence. Instead of simply using their emblems to maintain the community, the people of Zeal profited from their gifts, which had created a hierarchy of citizens based on the rarity and usefulness of their emblem. Their economy was one of the few things Tor had actually paid attention to in training, mostly because they had learned about it around the same time Engle had seen the frozen gnome in the city's markets.

At the very top of the settlement's system was its queen, Aurelia, born with an extremely rare form of the leadership emblem called the puppeteer. She had the gift not to inspire others to follow her lead, but to *force* them to.

Tor had heard stories about Queen Aurelia, but none of them were to be believed. The word of Zealite visitors could not be trusted, since the queen had the power to make them say what she pleased. But he did know this: she was a cruel leader who never had to follow any rules, even as a child. She had taken the throne at just thirteen years old.

Still, even though stories of visitors disappearing abounded, people continued to travel to Zeal for its markets. The bazaar was full of objects that had been enchanted with an emblem's power to do marvelous tasks—music boxes that could sing as well as Rosa, knives that could cut onions as expertly a Tor's father, shoes that could make the wearer dance like a master. Engle had returned from his trip to Zeal with a hydroclops statue that supposedly turned blue when danger was near, though there wasn't any way to prove its authenticity. Fake objects were about as plentiful as the real ones.

"Too bad I haven't got any dobbles on me," Engle said. "Could really use another statue. Think mine's broken."

Tor raised his eyebrows at him. "Engle, have you ever been in danger before today?"

He blinked. "Come to think of it, no." He reached deep into his pocket and pulled out the tiny snake figurine. "Though I suppose this little adventure of ours is the perfect opportunity to test it out."

"You carry that thing with you everywhere?" Melda asked, scrunching her nose in disapproval.

Engle shrugged. "Sometimes."

They headed toward Zeal's large gate, which stood open—though a few guards stood watch at the entrance, checking emblems. Those with marks that could deflect the queen's power were not permitted inside.

A flurry of worries suddenly bloomed in Tor's chest. He didn't *have* an emblem anymore. For the first time, Tor realized that he was now markless.

And then, of course, there was the curse.

At the very least, the dark markings on their wrists would make them appear suspicious. At the very worst...

It could get them imprisoned.

Tor walked toward the guards with trembling hands. Melda tried her best to twist her frown into a smile, and Engle's stomach chose that exact moment to groan like an angry giant.

Melda held out her arm and pulled up her sleeve, but just as she was about to be checked, the guard yawned. "Keep it moving," he said, bored, like he couldn't be bothered to take three children too seriously.

Fingers still shaking, Tor walked down the path in silence, not daring to say a word that might shatter their good luck. The walls echoed with bursts of sounds ahead. When they were far enough away, Tor released his hiked-up shoulders.

"You *know*," Melda said. "I'm not complaining, but you would think the queen would have better guards."

Engle rolled his eyes at her, and Tor was glad she didn't see it.

All at once, the narrow path opened up into a courtyard that made Estrelle's town square look about as impressive as a broom closet. Every Zealite was covered by color, hues Tor had never seen worn before: light purple on a little girl whose thick fabric coat looked nicer than anything he had ever owned, the pink of dusk on a woman's necklace, the shimmering gold of the sun on a man's feet, his shoes made of a material that seemed likely to melt in rain. Nothing like the primary colors favored by the people of Estrelle.

Engle grinned. "It's lightning, isn't it?" he said.

"A bit much was what *I* was thinking," Melda replied, arms crossed across her chest. In their village, her clothes were considered well-made, nicer than she could likely afford. Here, they looked downright ratty.

Tor stared down at his own clothes and felt plain. He suddenly—for just a moment—missed the purple rings around his wrist. The ones that made him special.

The ones Melda still wore. He caught a man staring at her wrist for a few seconds too long, eyes widened. Who knew what he, or others, would pay for a pinprick of its magic? A good leader's voice could incite hope, energy, and loyalty in a crowd more than anyone else's.

Melda quickly tugged down her sleeve. "Where's Engle?"

Tor turned and realized his friend had vanished. He

sighed. In a city with as many food carts as this one, it seemed he would have to watch Engle more carefully.

He took a long breath in and smelled something sweet and likely covered in frosting. They followed the scent, and, sure enough, they found Engle, trying to convince the woman at the cart to take his hydroclops statue in exchange for half a dozen diamond-dusted donuts.

She narrowed her eyes at him. "That thing might not even work," she said, then firmly shook her head no.

"Come on," Tor said, steering his crestfallen friend away. He had some money in his backpack, but the sweets stand was ridiculously overpriced, and who knew what else they might face on their way to find the Night Witch? He had to save his currency for an emergency.

Melda was busy studying the map. "Mrs. Libra told us that the Zealite know-all is the queen's adviser. So, to find him, I'm guessing we have to go there." She pointed straight up, which would have been strange if there hadn't been a building situated there. The city of Zeal was laid out in the shape of a spiral cone that resembled a hermit crab shell. The castle made up its point, a swirling tower that reminded Tor of a narwhal.

It looked so far up. *Too* far up.

To get there, it seemed like they would have to walk

around and around the spiral roads of the city. Getting to the top could take hours.

Like the courtyard, the spiral path to the tower was covered in stands, selling everything from super-bubble gum to enchanted lamps that lit up each time a specific person entered a room. Engle managed to stop at almost every booth, asking, "How much?" to each vendor, though he didn't have a single dobble in his pocket.

After a while, it became harder and harder for even Tor to focus on the reason they were there in the first place. The markets proved to be the ultimate distraction. He kept seeing trinkets Rosa would have loved, like a tiny paper bird enchanted to sing songs, or a paintbrush that drew pictures straight from a person's mind.

A group of children ran down the path, narrowly avoiding running into Tor. They held tiny sticks lit with fiery sparks that made popping sounds. Before the spark could reach the end, the kids raced to the edge of the street and threw their toys over the side. A moment later, there was a boom.

A bird made of fire appeared, a sparkler come to life. It flew over the crowd, just above their heads, feathers coated in flames. By the time it reached the opposite side of the city, it had disappeared in a puff of ash.

Tor turned and caught Melda looking amazed, her mouth

hanging open. She caught his gaze, and her expression promptly melted into a frown. "It's dangerous, you know. All of these enchantments running wild all over the city." Melda nodded toward Engle, a few stands away. "He thinks this is a game." She faced Tor again. "This is a nightmare."

Nightmare.

Just yesterday, he had thought *class* was a nightmare. Now, he realized he'd never known the meaning of the word.

A sharp jab to his ribs brought his attention back to Melda. "Tor," she was saying. "Tor, who is that?"

He looked up to see a group—no, a *procession*—heading their way. At the front was a tall, grasshopper-thin man who wore the most glorious gold wraps he had ever seen, made of silk so pure it looked like running water.

The people at the surrounding stands bowed, eyes to the ground. Tor looked to his left, where a group of children had kneeled. He noticed they were shaking, terrified.

Engle had his back to the approaching procession, still arguing with a vendor over the price of a multiplying muffin, when the man in gold planted a hand on his shoulder.

Tor gritted his teeth. This could not be good.

Surprisingly, he watched Engle break into a smile, say a few words, nod several times, then gesture toward his stomach. Melda sighed. After a few exchanged laughs, Engle turned around and motioned toward his friends. "Come on," he said, and they hesitantly walked over.

The man in gold turned and greeted them with a smile. He reached out his hand, and when Melda shook it, Tor noticed how carefully he studied her arm, like he was searching for her emblem.

"I'm Zeal's know-all, Jeremiah," he said brightly, and Tor raised his eyebrows. If the know-all dressed like this, he wondered what the queen wore.

The hesitation left Melda's brow as she broke into a relieved smile. "Of course," she said, nodding. "Of *course* you would know we were here." Tor didn't know why, but he was slightly annoyed at the awe that colored her tone.

Jeremiah grinned. "Yes, well, I do have my sources in the city. Come now, you've come a long way to find me." He motioned for the trio to follow, then turned around. Five guards flanked him on each side, moving as if they were connected by string. They wore full suits of armor, the metal reflecting all of the hues around them.

As they were led to the center of the spiral city, toward its stone core, Melda grinned at Tor, clearly convinced Jeremiah was the answer to all of their problems. Engle looked ready to burst from excitement, which likely had to do with some promise of food.

But Tor was reluctant. He didn't know how he could possibly trust someone who worked so closely with the puppeteer queen. Still, he resolved to keep an open mind. They *had* come a long way to find him, after all. They needed him.

It was with this attitude that Tor followed Jeremiah through a large gold door.

The doorway opened into a contraption that resembled a giant's cage. The box was big enough for all of them to fit inside and made completely of shining steel. As Jeremiah and the guards shuffled in, Tor held his friends back from the entrance, a worried look on his face.

The know-all smiled. "Don't be afraid," he said. "We can't be expected to *walk* all the way to the castle tower, can we?" He threw his arms up dramatically. "This is simply a more... efficient way of getting there."

Tor had to admit that his explanation made sense. He also knew that with ten armed guards present, they didn't seem to have much of a choice in the matter.

So he stepped forward. Once they were all through, one of the towering men promptly closed the door behind them, then reached toward a lever. Before Tor could ask what it was for, the large guard pressed down on the handle with all of his might, and they were off, shooting up like they had been thrown from a catapult.

Tor felt as though all of his organs were being thrown around his chest like fruits in a juggler's hands. His nails dug into his palms so forcefully he wouldn't have been surprised if they drew blood. He closed his eyes tightly, head spinning.

When they finally came to a stop, Engle was still screaming. Melda looked a ghastly shade of green.

Jeremiah smiled again. "You *must* get yourselves together," he said, rubbing a wrinkle out of his sleeve, then straightening his spine. "You're about to meet the queen."

"The queen?" Tor sputtered. He had assumed they were simply going to visit a library or the know-all's study.

"Why, of course. *No one* is allowed inside the tower without meeting her first. It's simply protocol. And I wouldn't cross her for the world."

"Of course," Melda replied merrily, though Tor noticed she had regained a bit of her previous hesitancy. Everyone knew of the queen's reputation. She could do to them what she pleased. The fact that Tor's mother was a chieftess meant nothing—they were in Aurelia's territory now.

The cage emptied out into a long hall that stretched in front of them in endless carpet. The walls were covered in paintings bigger than Engle and Tor stacked together, and they all had the same subject: the queen. Her long hair looked so blond it was almost white, and she wore an array of gold dresses that puffed up and out just like Tor's father's famous pastries. Their fabrics were laced with precious gems. Tor wondered how she possibly walked in gowns so heavy.

"Isn't she lovely?" the know-all asked, turning around to judge their expressions. They all nodded ferociously in reply.

Soon, they reached a pair of tree-sized doors. It took all ten guards to get them open just a crack...

And there she was.

The queen sat on a spiky throne made of the inside of a giant geode, her dress spilling around her in a stream of melted gold.

She looked up, her pouty mouth twisting into a smile. "Children!" she cried. "You've brought me children."

The know-all stepped forward and bowed so low his forehead almost hit the floor. "Yes, my queen. These are our visitors."

She snapped her fingers, and two guards, who had been standing at attention along the throne room's walls, hurried to the queen's side. Tor hadn't even noticed them when they first came in—their rich, gold uniforms so perfectly matched the textured gold wallpaper they had appeared to be part of the room itself. The guards gripped beneath her arms, and lifted her out of the chair, her heavy gown making it impossible to stand by herself.

"Visitors, hm?" she said, tapping a finger against her chin. "So many options." She started to laugh. "Shall I make you dance right off my marvelously high balcony? Fight each other to the death with the ruby-crafted swords from my collection?" She smiled merrily. "Come a little closer, won't you?" They didn't move an inch. One of her eyebrows rose. "No?"

The queen lifted her arm, and like their limbs were suddenly attached to strings, Engle, Melda, and Tor found themselves stumbling across the room toward her throne. When they were at Aurelia's feet, she dropped her hand, releasing her control. But not before Tor caught a glimpse of her emblem, two rings around her left wrist exactly like his had been, except gold instead of purple.

Sparks of anger traveled up and down his body. Those few moments under the queen's spell had made his stomach drop, his throat go dry. He had never felt so empty. So powerless. He had sensed Jeremiah meant trouble, and now the know-all had brought them right to a demented ruler, served up like a fine meal on a silver platter. They couldn't run, that was for sure. Queen Aurelia had proven she could simply drag them back if they tried.

They had to be smart, strategic. Everyone had a weakness.

Judging by the countless paintings in the hallway, Tor knew the queen's weakness must be herself. He bowed down low, then lifted his head. "Queen Aurelia, we are on a great quest and are here to seek your unmatched guidance and blessing."

Engle and Melda caught on quickly and hurried to bow down, too.

Her chin lifted just a smidge. "Is that so? I *am* very familiar with quests, you see. And I do have endless resources..." She squinted her caramel-colored eyes. "What is the purpose of your journey?"

"We aim to find the Night Witch."

The room became silent as a tomb.

And the queen looked suddenly very interested.

"The witch?" She leaned forward to such a degree that Tor wondered how she didn't fall. He supposed her gown acted as a counterweight.

He swallowed, wondering if the queen's reaction meant the story of the white-haired child could possibly be true. "The Night Witch."

The queen did not so much as blink. "And what is the purpose of your visit?"

He looked back at his friends, unsure of how much to reveal. Melda stepped forward. "We would like her to undo a curse."

The queen grinned, as if instead of *curse* Melda had said *carnival.* "How fun," she said, smacking her hands together and making them jump. "Well, what do you say we make a little deal?" She motioned toward Jeremiah. "I just so happen to have the best know-all in all of Emblem Island. He will give you the information you need to find the witch. *And* the tools you will require if you wish to survive the journey." Tor heard Engle gulp next to him. Aurelia regarded her nails, which looked as if they had been dipped in some sort of honey-thick dye. "Generous, I know."

Tor tried his best to look older, more mature. Shoulders set back and chin raised up. He knew enough about Aurelia to realize she wasn't doing anything out of the goodness of her heart. "And in return?"

"In return..." The queen smiled like there was a secret tucked between her lips. "I would like you to kill her for me."

Melda gasped. "Why?"

Aurelia raised her eyebrows, as if the answer was obvious. "She's a threat to my power, not to mention a danger in general. Many believe she is just a fairy tale. But I assure you, she is just as real as you or me." She sighed and regarded her nails again. "And killing her would really be a service to all of Emblem Island."

That might have been the truest sentence the queen had uttered. If such a person really existed, and the queen claimed she truly did, their island *would* be a far better place without the Night Witch around.

Still, as bad as she was rumored to be, Tor had never wanted to kill anyone. Even a person who had cursed him. He couldn't—he wouldn't. But it seemed as though the queen would not be giving them much of a choice.

"Unless, of course, you would prefer I make you spin in circles until your ears bleed, then take that one's pretty blue eyes for my own?"

Tor stepped forward before the queen could raise a finger. "No, we'll do it."

Aurelia's lips curled over her front teeth. "Excellent." She shifted her attention to Jeremiah. "Would you be so kind as to direct them to your study?"

He bowed. "Of course, my queen."

She batted them away. "Be gone."

The know-all's study was much more organized than the hermit's hut. Which, in truth, was not much of an accomplishment. Instead of piles, the room featured shelves built right into the walls, each filled with a collection of trinkets and books. Glass cases sat in the middle, and Tor guessed they housed Jeremiah's most prized relics.

A gold-woven basket held dozens of scrolls, positioned

vertically, with gems on their hilts. The know-all pulled out one with a sapphire top, unfurled it, made a few grunts that ranged from approval to wonder to surprise, then tapped at a spot. "This is where the Night Witch lives," he said.

Tor frowned. The know-all was not pointing to a specific place, but a large, dark, tornado-like hole that covered about a tenth of Emblem Island, beyond where Mrs. Libra's map even reached. The area was as big as twenty villages put together. And, unlike the rest of the page, nothing sat inside it, no city names or words. No castle from the last *Book of Cuentos* story. It was so bare the cartographer had chosen that exact location for the map's key, which held dozens of symbols meant to help the user distinguish a tree from a river.

It was the unknown parts of the island. The miles no one had written about.

"Um...could you be a bit more specific?" Melda said.

The know-all snapped the scroll closed with a satisfying *click*. "I'm afraid not. No one has actually found the Night Witch and lived to tell the tale. We have a *hintling* of where she might be, of course, but not an exact location. There are limits to even *my* knowledge." The man's tone dripped with regret, but Tor thought he didn't look sorry at all. In fact, he only seemed interested in staring at the spyglass symbol on Engle's arm.

His explanation made no sense. "If no one has lived to see her, how do you know she's even real?"

Jeremiah sighed. "Well, there are stories...legends that run deeper than the cracks in this heavy city's foundation. As soon as you enter the Shadows, the land beyond our maps' knowledge, it will be very clear that there's a...*force* behind the darkness. But don't take my word for it...no, no. Ten minutes in there and you'll see that I was right." His eyes became as still as a puddle. "You'll see I'm *always* right."

The Shadows. Where had Tor heard that before? He racked his brain, but couldn't find the answer, which irked him like an unreachable itch.

"By the Shadows, do you mean, like, from *Cuentos*?" Melda said.

"What do you mean?" Engle said, before the know-all could respond.

She shrugged. "In *The Book of Cuentos*, some monsters are described as living *in the shadows*. I always thought that meant behind an open door...or in a dark closet...or in an alleyway. But do you mean to tell me there's a *place* called the Shadows?"

The know-all made a face. "Of course." He clicked his tongue in a way that instantly became annoying. "Dear, *truly*, what kind of second-rate school are you in? Haven't your teachers ever taught you to read between the lines?"

Tor stiffened. "You're not saying those beasts are real, too?"

Jeremiah scoffed at him. "Of course that's not what I'm saying. What do you think I am, a court fool?" Tor's shoulders relaxed in relief as the know-all unfurled the map again. He studied it while humming an off-pitch melody. "*However*," he said, in almost a whisper. "You'll find most legends contain at least a grain of truth. Storytellers aren't creative enough to make it *all* up."

Melda tapped at a place on the map titled *Not-Very-Green Greenery.* "I've heard of this. It's a giant greenhouse filled with plants of unusual shades. Some plants with no shades at all. And then this place," she pointed to a village called Jade. "Everything *there* is green. How odd. If you look closely, it's almost like a pattern..." She dragged her finger across the map, all the way from Estrelle to the Shadows, and opened her mouth once more. But before she could speak, Jeremiah beat her to it.

"Good wish-god heavens, is there any school at *all* in your village? Don't answer that, of course I know that there is, I even know the names of your subpar teachers, but you would think your faculty was made up of squawking pelicans! You *do* know the rest of Emblem Island isn't as colorful as Estrelle and our great city of Zeal?"

Tor had never felt so clueless in his entire life. Of course he had heard of villages with *different* colors, but had never once learned about villages that weren't as colorful. He wasn't even sure what that meant.

The know-all sighed. "Apparently, I have to make this crystal clear..." He rolled his eyes. "The closer one travels to the Shadows, the less color they encounter. The nature there has shriveled up, most animals have abandoned its poisoned grounds. Living things no longer thrive. The journey will get darker and darker, quite literally, until you meet the Night Witch herself. That is, if you make it that far."

Melda held a hand up. "How can that be true? I've studied *hundreds* of treatises of villages and cities in Emblem Island and none—"

Jeremiah was quick to cut her off. "Described a place in the Shadows? A place fully without color? Not particularly surprising. A leader like you would never learn about a place with hardly any people to lead." He shrugged. "It really shouldn't be such a shock that you three don't know about the Shadows or the settlements around it. I'm quite sure not many people in your village have traveled far outside of its borders at all."

Tor gritted his teeth. Somehow, everything that came out of Jeremiah's mouth sounded like an insult.

Still, the know-all's words were not lost on him. He started to worry about practical things, such as food, water, and shelter. If no one lived in the dark corners of Emblem Island, where would they find resources?

Jeremiah handed Tor the map, which he quickly put into his backpack, shoved up against the other one. The know-all then turned, humming to himself. He looked as if he was about to reach into one of his glass cases, but stopped suddenly to stare at Melda.

No...at her necklace.

He grabbed the pendant between his fingers before she could tuck it away. "Great Zeal." Jeremiah's eyes were wide. "Your eyes, are of course, a very peculiar shade. I've only seen one other person with *that* color on their face. But this? This is downright priceless." He gave her an accusatory look. "How in the world did you come to possess a drop of color?"

Tor and Engle shared a shocked look. *That's* what that was? Drops of color were extremely rare—they could only be extracted by special creatures. The liquid from Melda's necklace could turn anything in the world that shade of blue.

Melda stared down at the ground sheepishly. "It's a family heirloom," she said, taking a step back so the necklace fell out of Jeremiah's hand.

Why didn't her family sell it, then? Tor wondered. They clearly needed the money.

The know-all opened his mouth to say something else

but then he seemed to think better of it, and cleared his throat instead.

"Well, I'll just state the obvious. The three of you are incredibly unequipped for a journey of this magnitude, I would wager you will all die a painful death at the hands of any number of threats you might encounter on the way. Also, by the looks of your lifelines, I would say you have at most a little more than a week of life left. I believe giving you this map and gift is as good as kissing them goodbye forever. A great and utter waste..."

He took a deep breath.

"*However*, the queen has spoken, and as her word is as good as law, I present you with this gift to help ease the pain of this impossible journey."

Jeremiah walked over to one of the glass display cases, slid open the top, then grabbed what sat inside: a dagger with a razor-thin edge and a single ruby on its silver hilt. He faced Tor. "A blade crafted out of the purest silver from the Alabaster Caves. The surest way to slay the Night Witch."

Tor swallowed, remembering his promise to the queen. He didn't want the weapon or the responsibility that came with it. But he took it anyway, slipping it into his pocket.

"And for you..." He turned to face Melda. He had a finger to his chin. "Well, I should say, and for *me*..."

"What?"

"I will be needing that drop of color, of course."

Melda looked at Engle and Tor, her head shaking ever so slightly as she took a step backward.

Jeremiah sighed. "Haven't you ever heard of reciprocity? I gave *you* a gift, and I expect one in return."

"No," Melda said firmly.

He grinned. "While I admire your boldness..." The know-all knocked against the wall, and footsteps sounded in the hall, along with clashing metal. "I wasn't asking."

Tor looked at Engle's pocket, where his friend's snake statue was poking out. It had turned a remarkable shade of blue.

Melda grabbed Tor's hand, and Tor grabbed Engle's. Just as the guards burst into the room, they ran toward the only other exit: the balcony door. They crashed through, the group of armed men right behind them, and only stopped when they reached the railing.

Engle gulped. "It must be, what? Five hundred feet down?"

"More like a thousand," Melda corrected.

By the time they turned back around, the guards had followed them outside, blocking the balcony door.

"There's nowhere for you to run," Jeremiah said. "I just want the girl. You two are free to go and complete the queen's task."

Tor stepped forward. "Never," he said. And he meant it.

The know-all shrugged. "Very well, then. Guards?"

The men stepped forward, swords drawn. Engle, Melda, and Tor pressed themselves against the banister, the sounds of the city far below—pops of sparkler animals, distant children's yells, and the chatter of haggling marketfolk. The know-all was right. There was nowhere to go.

Then, something peculiar happened. The lips on Engle's wrist parted and spoke just one word: "Jump."

And they did.

THE MARKLESS BOY

O nce upon a lilac dawn, there was a boy born markless—the only one in his family without an emblem.

Each night, he would go to the sea that bordered his home and pray. Wish for a power that would make him special. The coast bordering his village was supposed to be sacred, ever since a queen had walked into its waters and never returned, sacrificing her life for her child's.

He brought gifts for the water spirit. Golden apples, which bobbed on the sea's surface. Shells the color of sunset, which he had collected after a storm. Earrings he had taken from his mother's jewelry box, when she was not looking. But nothing worked.

One day, he found a child's toy—a doll—and offered that to the ocean.

The waters gleamed silver, and from its depths a woman appeared, glowing brighter than the moon behind her.

"I will grant you a single gift," she said, words

echoing across the sea. "One that will need to be earned."

"An emblem," he said desperately. "I will do anything for an emblem."

The sea spirit smiled. "I grant you a Grail. A quest that, if completed successfully, will earn you an emblem rarer than any other on the island. Are you up to this task?"

He said yes.

"I must warn you of many dangers. An almost certain death. And I offer a single comfort—the wish-gods will be watching. To save you once, should you need it."

He nodded solemnly. "I am up to this great task."

"Good. You may bring two others. They will be your comrades."

The boy knew exactly who he would take. His two brothers, who had fighting emblems and were always up for adventure.

"They, too, will be gifted glory, should they survive the journey."

"What is my quest?" he finally asked.

"Return this feather to the silver falcon," she said, as a plume floated toward him, landing in his palm. "So that he may roam the skies once more, whole, and able to help those in need of guidance."

7

CRISTAL TOWN

For a moment, they were falling. Engle was screaming. Melda was gasping. Then, she was grasping, catching a long, thin piece of fabric that hung in the air like a rope.

She held it tightly—then Tor, then Engle, hanging on for dear life, one swinging over the other.

They were floating.

Tor squinted up toward the sun and saw the top of their cord was a glorious red balloon the size of his house. It was a hopper, a balloon typically enchanted to take visitors to Zeal. He had no idea where it had come from but was grateful nonetheless. It took them up just far enough to see Jeremiah's shocked expression. And then they sailed away.

They broke through clouds, and Tor did his best not to look down, focusing instead on the threads from the fabric that had magically wrapped around and around his hand, keeping him attached. He felt the weight of the dagger still in his pocket, its tip poking through the fabric and grazing his leg each time the balloon lurched in a different direction. They flew until the tall city of Zeal was blocked by even larger mountain ranges.

He finally glanced toward his feet, and saw them kicking over thin air. Far below, fields cut into different-colored squares sat, looking very much like his grandmother's quilts. It was a strange feeling, flying. Tor had expected it to be freeing, but found it was the exact opposite. He had never felt so chained to an object as he did now, his sweaty fist tied to the balloon's string.

He shook his head in disbelief. They had just jumped off a balcony! What were they thinking? Worse, when the lips on Engle's wrist had spoken, he hadn't even given it a second thought. He had simply acted. Was he losing his mind?

They were getting more reckless by the minute.

Still...though it felt like he could fall hundreds of feet at any moment, Tor couldn't help but smile.

Yes, he was most definitely losing his mind.

The balloon began to lower. Tor watched the ground get closer and closer, rushing toward him, the roar of the wind making his ears itch and nose go numb, until his feet were on solid earth once again, and the string released its hold. He fell forward, off-balance, landing on his stomach, and relished the feeling of dirt against his cheek. Melda, then Engle, joined him moments later.

The balloon broke through the clouds, disappearing from view.

After recovering from bouts of dizziness and letting their rapidly beating hearts settle down, Engle, Tor, and Melda gathered together. They all stared at the same thing—the lips on Engle's wrist.

"It spoke," Melda said firmly.

Engle looked up at her. "Well, we *know* that."

Who had spoken was the mystery. Who had helped them?

Tor pressed his mouth into a line. One possibility came to mind, but it was very nearly impossible. Still, he couldn't resist throwing it out there. "Well, you know, I *am* technically markless."

"So?" Engle said.

"If the Night Witch is real, then maybe some of the other legends are true, too. The ones told on the nights before Eve, in particular."

Melda blinked. "You don't actually think—"

Engle snapped his fingers. "Of course!" A giddy smile spread across his freckled face. "Well, this makes things interesting."

Melda shook her head. "But those things aren't even real."

Engle smirked. "Well, we didn't think curses were real, did we?"

"I suppose so, but—"

"But what? Tor has been sent on a quest! A *Grail*." They had read stories of Grails in *Cuentos*—devised by the wish-gods to give markless children a chance at earning an emblem. And not just any emblem, but a marking that was one of a kind.

These quests were not easy, Tor knew. Legends of Grails were full of man-eating monsters and long travels. Most did not make it very far, given the risks. Life on Emblem Island for the emblem-less was bad enough to make it worth it, however.

Still, to give them a chance at success, in *Cuentos*, children on a Grail were often helped by the same spirits that granted wishes on Eve: the wish-gods. The voice that had spoken through the mouth on Engle's skin must have been one of them.

Engle paced around the field they had landed in and threw his hands up. "It all makes sense. Your Grail must be to defeat the Night Witch. Once you do, who knows what kind of emblem you'll be gifted!"

Tor felt excited, but also like he was about to be sick. Engle's eyes widened, and he made an excited expression usually reserved for especially good bites of cake. "And *we're* your comrades!" In each old quest tale, the markless child was assisted by two especially gifted partners, called comrades. If their quest was successfully completed, they, too, enjoyed fame for ages.

Melda didn't look convinced. "Well, Grail or not, one thing is for sure. If we don't find the witch soon, we'll all be dead." She held up her shortened lifeline to drive her point home.

Daylight was fading. Soon, a carpet of stars would be blinking back at them. Tor's grandmother used to say the nighttime sky was simply sparkling fabric that could be cut into pieces. She told stories of a seamstress who had a ladder so tall she could climb to the heavens, cut the stars into cloth, and use it to make the most beautiful dresses.

By the time Tor had started training, and the fairy tales from *The Book of Cuentos* had been revealed to be silly lies, he had felt foolish for once believing his grandmother's stories.

Perhaps he should have listened to them more carefully.

"We'll have to find food and shelter for the night. Tomorrow, we set off toward the Shadows."

The red balloon had dropped them off just a mile short of Cristal Town.

Tor's allowance was enough for a warm meal at Pasty Pub, a narrow light purple building squeezed in between the town's bank and theater. They ate quickly—except for Engle, who ordered two more rounds of pie, gifted to him by the sympathetic bar owner. The woman took pity on them once again and offered a room for a quarter of the price. Tor fell asleep to the faint sound of an opera show next door. His dreams were dark and full of shadows.

Down to his last dobble, the next day's breakfast consisted of stale pastries for half-price and a few canteens of water they stored in Tor's backpack, which had become harder to zip—and carry. Now that they had Jeremiah's map, Tor decided to trade the hermit's for two loaves of bread and a block of cheese, which the pub owner wrapped in paper, before retreating into the kitchen.

Tor pulled the remaining map out of his backpack. "I've been thinking," he said.

Melda smirked. "Great, that's just what we need. Another idea from you. What did you wish for this time? A plague?"

He ignored her and rolled open the scroll so that it covered the length of the bar. "Emblem Island is bigger than we knew. Whichever path we take, making it here," he pointed to the large dark hole that was the Shadows, "Will take days. Five if we're lucky. Possibly six. Not a lot of room for error."

"What are you getting at?" Engle asked, trailing a finger across his empty plate.

"If we don't take the exact right way, we'll be dead before we ever find the Night Witch."

Melda sighed. "All right, but what choice do we have? We don't know the exact right way. We have just the faintest idea of where she lives."

The night before, Tor dreamt of monsters that hadn't filled his nightmares in years—not since he was Rosa's age. Though he had woken up covered in sweat and panting like he had run a mile, those dreams might have been a blessing. They had given him an idea. "Jeremiah said no one has ever found the Night Witch and lived." He pulled something out of his bag and dropped it onto the table with a thump. "But what if someone has?"

The Book of Cuentos sat before them, the copy the hermit had given Tor. The silver-piped cover caught the light coming from the pub's single, dust-glazed window. It gleamed, almost like a wink.

"Whoever wrote this book might be the only one who met the witch and lived to tell the tale. The storyteller traveled across Emblem Island, and in the end found the Night Witch. Think of the storyteller not as a writer...but as an explorer." Tor closed his eyes and swallowed, knowing he was about to sound as nutty as a cashew. "What if we treated this book as less of a collection of stories and more as a map to her?"

Engle blinked. "How would we do that?"

Tor opened the book and scanned one of its first tales.

"There," he said, sticking his finger right in the middle of one of the legend's last paragraphs. "The husband and wife were turned into a giant snake with one head at each end. Forever connected."

"They turned into a hydroclops," Engle said excitedly, nodding. "A cousin of the two-headed wrangler worm. A bit deadlier, I would say. Makes an anaconda look like a caterpillar."

Melda thrummed her nails against the bar. "What in the world does that have to do with finding the Night Witch?"

Tor took a deep breath. He hoped his plan sounded better out loud than it did in his head. "If we can find parts of these stories that match up with places on this map—geographical features, names, descriptions, animals, anything—then it might lead us directly to the witch. She's the last chapter, after all, 'The Night Witch's Castle.' We can follow the storyteller's path through the island right to her."

Engle sighed. "There are dozens of stories in the book, though. That would take forever."

Tor had thought of that, too. But he had an idea. "What if we only followed the monster myths?" Though there were many chapters in *The Book of Cuentos*, only a handful described the origin of wicked creatures, the monsters Tor and Engle had been fascinated with for years. "The Faceless Man," "The Weeping Woman," "The Night Witch," even.

"But how do we know the person who wrote *Cuentos*— the storyteller—even started his book on this side of the island?" Engle brought up a good point. The storyteller could have started his travels at the very southern tip of Emblem Island, in Manzana, where caves made up the coast. Or even the fishing town of Perla, a city known for its harbors.

"The very first story is in Estrelle," Tor said, referring to the tale about their village's founder, one he had always thought had been a lame attempt at explaining why Estrelle was so colorful. Now that the chapters in *Cuentos* didn't seem so far-fetched, Tor realized the storyteller was really more of a collector, gathering the island's stories on his travels and writing them down.

"*Think of the storyteller not as a writer, but as an explorer*," Melda repeated. She squinted down at the parchment. "So, you're saying if we can figure out where the first creature origin story supposedly took place, where the hydro-clops lives..."

"Then that's the first step to finding the Night Witch."

"Brilliant," Melda said, looking surprised. Her nose then

pointed toward the ceiling. "If you're right about this storybook being a sort of map, that is." She turned to Engle. "Well, you fancy yourself as an animal expert. Where on Emblem do we find this snake?"

Engle bit at the side of his lip and made a low grunting sound. "Well, the hydroclops is an amphibian, and it needs a wet, swamp-like environment—its scales need to be moistened every few hours. They don't do well in direct sunlight, either. Their giant eyes must be quite sensitive to it..." He looked deep in thought. "I'd say we'd find the creature in a heavily shaded, extremely wet area. A tropical one."

"Somewhere like this?" Melda said. Her finger hovered over a place on the map northeast of Cristal Town, painted vibrant green. A rain forest called Zura.

"Exactly like that."

Melda's smug expression faltered. She blinked a few times too many. "From my understanding, rain forests are filled with all sorts of...*murderous* specimens," she said. "Can't we just go around it, to the next stop?" She cleared her throat. "For logistical reasons, of course."

Tor wished they could. He had thought of the same thing. "Given our time constraints"—his gaze drifted toward his shortened lifeline—"going around Zura will take too long. Going *through* is the fastest way." Melda still did not look convinced.

"Even if we figured out the Night Witch's castle's location and skipped everything else, it would be a bad idea to veer from the storyteller's path. The monsters from these stories are terrible enough, but at least we know what we'll be dealing with. If we go any other way, we could encounter creatures we've never heard of, ones we don't know how to get past."

"Tor, if we go *toward* all of these *Cuentos* beasts, then we're dead! There's no way we can—"

"Melda," Tor said steadily. "We're dead if we don't try." The truth of that statement made his throat go dry.

"Very well," Engle said, getting up from his chair and rubbing his backside. They had been seated on the tiny bar stools for quite some time. He smiled, looking not the least bit worried. In fact, he looked downright excited. "Let's go monster hunting."

●)) (

Before leaving Cristal, Melda stopped in front of a shop at the edge of town. "We're going to need something," she said, turning to Engle with her hand outstretched. "May I see your snake statue?"

He looked horrified and shot a protective hand into his pocket. "What for?"

"We don't have any dobbles left. I'm going to try to make another trade."

Engle took a few steps back. "Oh no you're not, not with my figurine."

Melda gave him a look. "Don't act so attached. You were ready to part with it for a half dozen donuts in Zeal."

Engle squinted. "Are you trading it for food?"

"No."

"Then I don't think so."

Melda crossed her arms and sighed like an impatient teacher getting ready to explain a lesson for the fifth time. "The only way we make it across this island is with a compass." She pointed to a particularly nice one in the shop window. "So, again, I'm going to need that statue."

Engle swallowed. "We can't trade it," he stammered. "How—how are we going to know if we're in danger?"

"We're chasing monstrous creatures across a land we know almost nothing about, in order to find a witch." She took a breath. "I think it's safe to say that for the next few days, we'll *always* be in danger."

Melda was right. They needed a compass. Tor gave Engle a sharp nod, and his friend bit his lip. "Fine," he said, handing the snake statue over while looking in the opposite direction.

"Thank you very much," Melda said, feigning gratitude.

"Let's hope this piece of junk is worth something." She skipped away before Engle could yell anything after her.

She was back a minute later.

"Turns out your little figurine was worth a lot more than we thought, outside of the city of Zeal. Got a compass *and* this light bulb." An orb sat on her palm, enchanted with light stolen right from the sun.

She handed it to Engle to hold, and he looked a little less miserable.

They set off into the woods in the northeast direction, leaving the village and its people behind.

Engle scraped his teeth against a piece of bread from the pub, trying to make it last longer. "Hard as a rock," he said, then looked over at Melda and Tor. "Let me know if you don't want yours." He continued to make scraping noises over the next half hour, until he gave up and shoved the rest of the roll right into his mouth. It cracked so loudly that Tor wondered if Engle had chipped a tooth. "How far are we?" he asked.

It was late morning, and the sun was beginning to be uncomfortably bright. The pale, sparse trees did little to block its rays. Tor's head felt like it was on fire, and the spot on the very top of his skull was especially tender.

He looked down at the map. "Should only be another hour or so."

Engle groaned. Now he held the block of cheese. "If only one of us was a telecorp, right? That would be a lightning emblem to have... We wouldn't even have to walk, we could just teleport everywhere, even a few feet away."

He looked at Melda like he expected her to respond. She didn't.

"We need to move faster," Tor said. He wanted to add that Melda's slug-like pace wasn't doing them any favors, but didn't want to be the recipient of another one of her frosty glares.

They took turns carrying the backpack, which had been made heavy by their map, the book, food, and dagger.

Dagger. Thinking about its purpose made chills creep down Tor's spine.

He jumped, startled, as Melda yelled out.

"These are moraberries," she shouted from a few yards away, reaching toward a spiky shrub. "We read about them once, Tor, remember? They're quite valuable to the Balayas, based in a village to the south, I believe. Makes up almost their entire currency." Tor, as a matter of fact, did not remember. Which was probably because he had never read the assignment in the first place.

Melda picked dozens of the purple fruits, their pale, sickly color hardly looking like food to Tor. Actually, it looked as though they had soured ages ago. Engle apparently didn't care about their strange shade, because he grabbed five at once and threw them all into his mouth. His eyes immediately bulged. "These are sweeter than rubies," he declared, then plucked off more, until the entire bush was bare. Then, he reached toward Melda's stash, and she pulled them away, carefully placing the berries into a worn-looking handkerchief. "These are for later."

Engle looked upset until he turned back around. "Whoa."

Tor saw nothing but rows of the same pale trees. A few minutes later, however, he discovered what sharp-eyed Engle had been admiring.

At the forest's edge sat a rolling field of pasty flowers. They were every color of the rainbow, but slightly more muted than what they would see in Estrelle. Tor admitted that though they looked strange, drained of color like a tapestry left too long in the sun, they were beautiful in their own way. He had never thought of Melda as the flower-picking type, but there she was, grabbing as many as she could, until she held a large bouquet. She tied the stems together, expertly twisting them into an elaborate knot, then put them into his backpack.

"Saving the color for later," she explained. "For when we enter the Shadows and there's no color at all."

Before long, the flowers disappeared, covered by grass so long and lush it looked like combed-over fur. It grazed their ankles and trembled gently in the breeze.

"Here we go," Engle said as they approached a line of trees thick and tall like a rampart wall. Their trunks reached two hundred feet into the air, making Tor feel about the size of a fire ant. "Being alive was nice."

"Being alive was nice," Tor repeated, and they stepped inside.

8

ZURA

The first thing that struck Tor about the rain forest was the lack of sunlight—one moment they were drowning in gold, and the next, every ounce of radiance was ripped away. He craned his neck and did not see a single pocket of light shining down, the sun wholly blocked by treetop canopies that merged to form a ceiling, like thousands of umbrellas pressed together.

Then, there was the silence. No person lived here, Tor thought, that was for sure. He wondered if perhaps the animals had found their own faraway, hidden patches of the forest, or if they were simply watching the three of them as they stepped over creeping vines with the care of true tourists.

They walked for several minutes, the quiet only finally interrupted by what sounded like the howl of a strange bird. No, not a bird...something else.

"That's a monkey," Engle said. He squinted and turned in all directions, searching the branches. "There!"

Tor strained his eyes, but saw nothing. It must have been too far away.

He wondered what else he couldn't see.

"Get down!" Engle yelled, dragging his friends to the ground. Part of Tor's cheek stung where it made contact with a jagged pebble in the dirt, but he did not feel to see if it was bleeding.

A bird with a wingspan the size of three houses had nosedived through the trees, and now hovered just above them, gray-blue feathers looking like melted moonlight. The creature's neck extended two yards away from its body, writhing unnaturally from side to side.

"Don't move," Engle whispered from his place next to Tor, all three of them pressed against the ground. Tor's head was turned to the side, just inches away from a talon the size of a boat anchor, sharp enough to tear right through him.

The creature floated over them for a few minutes, the beating of its wings producing gusts of wind that rustled their hair and blew dirt into their faces. And then, with an angry squawk, it left.

They waited a while before getting up, as Engle warned them it might return. He whispered that birds of prey often pretended to leave, so that their victims came out of hiding. Then, just when their target believed the coast was clear, the beast would swoop in for the kill.

It was almost half an hour later before they finally got up, and Melda was still shaking.

"I've never seen... That *thing*... Its claws! Did you see its..." She trailed her nails through her hair, making it even more knotted on the top, hyperventilating enough that Tor thought she might just fall over. Melda turned to Engle with wide, blinking eyes. "If it wasn't for you," she said. "We'd be skewered!"

Engle shrugged in response. "It's a little too early for us to die a painful death, don't you think?"

Tor nodded. And, even though all he wanted was to run straight out of the rain forest, he started through the tangle of trees once more. "What was that thing?"

"Harpy owl," Engle said. "Nasty creatures. Known for cutting their prey clean in half with their talons. There's likely a nest of them somewhere in the treetops."

Nest? It would have to be as big as their entire village square to hold a mess of beasts like that, Tor thought.

"Well, good thing it's still daytime," Melda said. "Wouldn't want to be running across the likes of *that* in the dead of night."

Very quickly, day turned to dusk. With darkness came various nighttime sounds; Tor imagined many of the animals in the rain forest were nocturnal—some creature howled at the moon, another made a noise like a fist knocking against a door, and then there was the animal that sounded unlike anything Tor had ever heard. Almost like a sneeze, or a strange sort of cough. He wondered if even Rosa could mimic these odd creatures.

But it wasn't just the animals that were peculiar... No, even the plants and trees looked like they belonged on a different planet. Every time he turned around, there was something new: a long petal that curled and uncurled like a scroll; a sunflower that stood as tall as his house; an apple tree so small it could fit into his palm; a plant with leaves that looked very much like red lips; one that seemed to have a row of teeth...

And then they came upon a flower with a bulb bigger than Tor's entire body. It was closed up for the night, pointed toward the sky. He wondered how it lived with so little sunlight, then lifted a finger to touch its tip, curious.

Suddenly, it bloomed.

Its petals opened as large as palm fronds, long and thick and smooth. But the plant's size was, strangely, its least unusual attribute.

The flower was *glowing*. The purple and green dots that spotted its body shined brightly through the darkness.

"What in the—" Before Melda could finish her sentence, the world around them changed. All at once, almost every herb and shrub, down to the weeds, illuminated in fluorescent colors.

And it was not just the plants.

A monkey swung right in front of Tor's face, holding on to a shining green vine, and *it* had spots of glowing pigment, a string of bright yellow dots trailing down its curled-up tail. Even the tree roots, which ran across the dirt in spiderweb patterns, glowed green.

Engle threw his hands up, exasperated. "We're officially the most boring things in this rain forest," he said before breaking into a wicked grin. "Let's change that."

He took off at a run. Tor followed, and then Melda, who yelled at their backs.

"This is dangerous!"

They kept going.

"We need to consult the map!"

Tor did not so much as turn around.

"Fine, I hope you both get eaten by a giant glowing cockroach!"

They jumped over vines, narrowly avoided smacking into trees, and ducked just in time to dodge a ten-foot-long spider, whose legs shined bright blue. Engle led the way, his vision no doubt searching for which direction held the greatest wonders. He did not stop until they reached a lake.

It was covered in giant water lilies with curved-up edges, big enough to sleep on. They floated in place, rocking gently from side to side.

Melda seemed to know what Engle was about to do before he took a single step forward. "Don't you dare!" she yelled.

But he did anyway.

Engle jumped onto the first giant water lily, and Tor watched it turn purple, for just a moment. When his friend moved to another lily, it, too, changed shade, then settled back to green. Engle jumped merrily from one to the next, until he was halfway across the pond. "Come on!"

Tor shrugged, and leapt forward, landing right in the middle of the lightweight plant. It drifted a few feet, and, when it was close enough, he jumped to the next, watching it bloom violet. For a moment he wondered what lurked in the dark pool below. It seemed like forever since he'd gone for a swim...

He froze. A long, slithering creature moved through the water beneath him, its back a myriad of neon shades.

"They're electric eels!" Engle yelled from a few lilies ahead. "Nutty, right?"

Tor turned back toward shore, only to see Melda sticking a pointed toe toward one of the floating plants, the rest of her body firmly on the ground. "Jump, or you'll tip it over," he called out. He could see the fear painted across her face even from far away. "It's fun," he added, surprising himself with the patience in his voice. "Nothing to be afraid of."

Before he knew it, Melda scurried back a few paces, then broke into a run. She jumped and landed directly atop one of the lilies on her hands and knees, with enough force that she went soaring down the stream, past Tor.

Melda turned and gave him a sheepish smile.

They all ran side by side, leaping across the pond, the lilies glowing in a purple path behind them. Flowers the size of Tor's family's dinner table floated at the fringes of the lake, their white, rose-like petals opening wide, as if basking in the limited moonlight.

By the time they made it across, Melda, Tor, and Engle were laughing, holding the sides of their stomachs to keep them from cramping.

"I saw a huge turtle with a red swirl on its shell," Engle said.

"Oh yeah? I saw a fish with skin like a tree," Melda countered.

"A bark-back bass?" Engle asked.

Tor grinned. "Say that three times fast."

"Bark-back bass, bark-back bass, bark-back bass," Engle said excitedly, as he rushed back to the edge of the water, likely to catch a glimpse of it.

Tor spotted a strange, transparent-looking plant a few feet away. It laid on its side, long and hollow, as large as a tunnel. He stepped inside, and the bottom crunched, like the crinkle of dead leaves. It was as if the plant had scales, or at least the imprint of them.

"Do you know what plant this is?" he called out, turning to face Engle.

When his friend saw the tunnel, his face lit up in delight—then quickly dimmed. "It's...um...not a plant." He gulped. "It's skin."

Tor's brow ruffled. "Skin?" He poked at the substance, and tore a hole right through. "What kind of—"

Oh.

He jumped out of the tube as quickly as he could, stepping his way back toward his friends. If he was right, that was *snakeskin*, and there was only one serpent big enough to have shed a hull he could have walked through.

"Do you hear that?" Melda asked in a tiny voice.

Tor did hear that; he knew the sound better than most.

Something was moving through the water.

A serpent swam toward them with the speed of a

lightning bolt, brightly colored diamond shapes running down the length of its spine. Within seconds, it crossed the entire pond. No—it was almost as *long* as the entire pond. It had simply surfaced from depths deep below...

The hydroclops lifted out of the water with the burst of an explosion, both heads emerging side by side. They stood fifty feet into the air, forked tongues shooting in and out of their identical mouths. The two sides of the serpent turned to look at each other, then at them.

"Run!" Engle yelled. They took off, and within a moment, the snake was at their feet. "Split up!"

Melda and Engle went left, and Tor went right. Just as he entered the trees, Tor turned to see that each head had attempted to chase its own target, slowing the creature down. The beast would have to decide which end would lead and which would be the tail, which meant Tor had about five seconds to get as far away as possible.

Tor ran faster than he ever knew he could, thorned plants cutting his ankles. He shoved glowing green vines out of his way, but there were too many. One hit him on his side and almost knocked him down with its force, the vine as thick as a broadsword. He popped up and kept going. Plants that had slept peacefully now bloomed brightly at both of his sides, coming to life at his proximity, then closing once he passed.

His breathing became rugged, loud; his legs burned beneath him, their muscles being pulled in all sorts of directions as he jumped over stumps and through a labyrinth of trees.

Tor ran so quickly that when the ground suddenly curved down, his foot missed its next step, and he fell, rolling as quickly as a barrel down a waterfall, only seeing flashes of green and brown as he plunged down the slope.

By the time he came to a stop, everything hurt. His ribs were tender, his knees burned, his head flashed in pain.

He heard a scream—*Melda*. A moment later, she and Engle rolled down the same hillside, until they were just a few yards to his right.

The hydroclops broke through the trees. Just one head poked out first, and then the other followed, the creature curved into a u-shape. Tor walked sideways until he reached his friends, and the three of them huddled together, stepping backward until there were no more steps to take. They had run right into a tree trunk as thick as the snake itself.

The serpent curved its two heads down to their height, four giant nose holes breathing steam right into their faces. Engle coughed and Melda whimpered. "What do we do?" she whispered.

"Die," Engle said, his voice trembling. "I think we die."

One of the beast's mouths opened unnaturally wide, its fangs as big as their legs, and moved to strike—

But before it could, they heard a cracking sound like hundreds of branches being snapped in half.

The snake's heads lurched back, turning toward the noise, just as something a hundred feet tall broke off from the side of one of the tallest trees.

"What is that?" Melda whispered.

Engle grabbed them each by the wrist. "Who cares? It's distracted."

Just as they turned to run, a boy around their age with what looked like paint smeared across his body stumbled out of the brush. "Come with me," he said.

Melda was the first to follow.

"Shouldn't we ask who this person is?" Tor asked Engle as they trailed the boy through the glowing vegetation. Close up, Tor could see animals painted across his body—a purple-striped tiger on his forearm, an orange snake on his leg, a green spider on his stomach. Tor counted ten images then kept finding more, the boy's skin almost as colorful as the forest around them. They weren't emblems, *no*, but something else: a man-made marking.

Engle shrugged. "We just barely escaped being eaten whole. I'd follow just about anyone."

They reached a thick tree with a red dot painted on its base. Deep indentations in the bark made a sort of ladder that wrapped around the entire trunk, all the way to the top.

"Come on." The boy scurried up the tree with the ease of a squirrel.

Normally, Tor would have been a bit more afraid of heights. But at that moment, he was just happy to be off the creature-infested ground.

The climb up was astounding—each ten feet was like entering a new world—with different colors, patterns, and animals, who had each seemingly claimed their own layers of the rain forest.

They kept going, climbing more than two hundred feet up, and Tor wondered where the boy could possibly be leading them. Only when they reached the very top did they stop.

And that was when Tor heard voices. Just above, a few feet away...

He poked his head out of the treetop and gasped.

This was why they hadn't encountered another human until now. The Zura village did not exist on the ground, or even in the trees, but *over* the treetops, far above the deadly creatures that roamed below.

There were homes in the distance, with giant palm fronds for roofs and bark for doors, tied together by rope bridges. There was a market, selling everything from choco-late to expertly woven baskets to necklaces made of teeth large enough to be fingers. Strings of lights hung between the huts, made of tiny orbs, the same type that villagers in Estrelle sometimes strung on the trees that jutted out of their houses. Nearby, someone roasted a giant red pepper on a spit, charring its skin. Next door, a man sold curled cinnamon sticks that bathed the night air in spice, the smell reminding Tor of the traditional Eve tea his father always made.

He had surfaced right in front of a stand selling bunches of bananas by the barrel. "Get them before the monkeys do!" the vender yelled out.

"What is this place?" Melda asked.

"We call it the Canopy, just a small part of Zura," the boy replied. "And I'm Koso." He hauled himself up, then walked over to the merchant. "Three cocoanuts for my new friends, here. They just survived the hydroclops."

They each stared down at the nuts in wonder. "Thank you?" Tor said.

Engle shook his next to his ear.

Koso laughed. "Here," he said, before taking three metal straws from the vender's stand. He sharply stuck one into Tor's cocoanut. "Drink," he instructed.

Tor did, and sipped the sweetest chocolate-flavored milk

he had ever tasted. His throat dry from their journey, he drank and drank, until his straw scraped against the bottom of the empty nut.

Koso sat cross-legged directly on top of the tree they had just climbed, which was surprisingly steady, and patiently waited for them to finish. When Melda finally put her drink down, he cleared his throat. "Now," he said. "What in the world are you three novates doing out here?"

Tor figured *novate* was a term for outsider...and also sensed that the Zurians did not frequently happen upon them.

Melda told Koso their story, starting from the night of Eve. Even though she went on for too long, drawing out unimportant parts, Koso listened intently, only interrupting when Engle started to slurp loudly at a clearly empty cocoanut.

"If you want another one, just ask," Koso said. And Engle did ask. Several times.

Melda finally concluded her tale with a long sigh. "Any questions?"

Koso pursed his lips. "Just one." He turned to Tor. "How could you not believe in the Night Witch?" He shook his head. "In Zura, legends are as good as law."

"You know of her?"

"Of course. We have a different name for her here, but it's

the same being." He shrugged. "I might be able to help you find your next location, if you would like me to take a look."

Tor immediately pulled out the book from his backpack, flipping through stories until he reached the next one, called "Melodines and Captivates." He skimmed the beginning and remembered that melodines lived in oceans. They weren't anywhere near a sea and didn't have time to go all the way up to the coast... He flipped to the next tale: "The Pelilargas." Koso read over his shoulder.

"No more!" A yell from the fruit stand made Tor jump. "This boy is going to put me out of business!" The merchant sent Engle away after he tried to claim his seventh cocoanut.

Koso sat back on his arms, looking pensive. Chico had emerged again and sat on Koso's shoulder. "I've never heard this tale and don't know where to find these...*charming* characters," he said.

Great, Tor thought.

"But I might know somebody who does."

"Do they live around here?" Melda asked, excitedly looking around the Canopy.

Koso grinned. "Not exactly. But I know a highly efficient way of getting there."

"No. There is absolutely no *way* I'm getting on that." Melda stood with her arms crossed. "It's a death trap! I don't do death traps."

Tor turned to Koso. "Are you sure this is safe?"

Koso raised his eyebrows, looking confused. "Of course it's not safe."

Melda's mouth dropped open. "You see! He just said—"

Koso held up a finger. "*But*, in Zura people use them to get around every day. There's only been one death this year. Okay, maybe two—actually three, if you count Eve. Anyway..." He swung one arm around Tor and the other around Melda, who had paled. "If you follow my lead, you'll be fine."

Follow my lead. Even though Tor no longer had a leadership emblem, the idea of following anyone other than himself—and, okay, maybe his mother—seemed strange. But he guessed he needed to learn to trust other people.

"If it's the fastest way through the rain forest, then we should go," he said. Melda swung around to face him, shocked. He shrugged. "It could buy us some time."

Engle did a little dance. "Yes! I get to go first. All right, second. Koso should probably lead the way. But I definitely don't want to go last."

They were inside a small hut, positioned near the top of a tree, standing on a wooden platform. Above them ran a wire that dipped down at a forty-five-degree angle, looking both steady and frighteningly thin. A rusted pulley and red handle attached to the cable, swinging gently in the night breeze.

Tor squinted, trying to see where the wire went, but he couldn't. It disappeared into the thicket of trees and could have ended up just about anywhere. "What do you call this?" he asked Koso.

"There are several names. Some people call it the death slide. Others, a zippy."

Melda gave him a look. "Death slide?"

Koso grinned. "Don't worry, as long as you don't let go, you'll be fine." He pursed his lips, looking thoughtful. "And, as long as a hawk doesn't sweep in on you from above. Or, a horned-toe gorilla doesn't happen to be swinging through the trees at the exact moment you're passing through... They *do* like to hunt at this time of night." He sighed. "But that would just be terrible luck and is highly unlikely."

Tor grimaced. "I think you should stop talking," he suggested.

Koso nodded. "Less talking, more zipping. I like it."

"No, I didn't mean—"

The Zurian boy jumped to grip the handle, swinging a few times back and forth. Then, he turned around and winked. "See you on the other side!" he yelled, before kicking off from the wooden platform. In a whoosh, he was gone, disappearing like he had jumped right through a cloud.

The three remaining handles swung side to side, taunting them.

"Well, I'm off," Engle said, grasping the next one. He sailed down and away.

Melda shook her head. "I'm not going, do you hear me? That treacherous balloon ride was bad enough, but falling through a forest full of creatures that want to have me for dinner? No way." She turned to Tor. "You'll just come find me? You'll come back for me after you've found this person Koso knows, after you've figured out where we're going next?"

Tor swallowed. "You know we can't do that," he said gently. "We'll lose too much time."

She stomped her foot. "And what if we get eaten by that horrible harpy bird from before? We won't have much time then!" Her hiked-up shoulders slumped abruptly. "Aren't you afraid?"

"Of course I'm afraid," he said louder than he meant. He cleared his throat. "I've been afraid since the moment I woke up with this." He motioned his chin toward the eye sitting calmly on his wrist.

She made a grumbling noise, then sighed, long and heavy. Finally, she held her head high. "You'll be right behind me?"

Tor nodded solemnly, passing Melda her handle. "Close

your eyes," he whispered. "Imagine you're somewhere else—imagine you're flying." She shut her blue eyes tightly, tucked her necklace safely away, and nodded. Swallowed. Kicked off the platform...

And then she was falling, screaming so loudly a dozen tiny birds shot out of the neighboring tree.

"Being alive was nice," Tor said to himself, before taking his own handle, saying a little prayer to the wish-gods, and hoping his next step wouldn't be his last.

Tor quickly realized why the terrifying contraption was called a zippy. That was the noise the pulley made against the wire as he flew through the rain forest, fast as a sailfish. His stomach was in his throat, his heart lodged somewhere above that, every drop of the cable stirring up a new batch of nausea.

Something bright purple whizzed by his left ear, missing his skin by just inches. Then, something below him, swinging through the trees. He wondered if he should follow his own advice and close his eyes, and as soon as he did, he found it was so much worse.

He opened one eye again, just a crack—and at that exact moment, a bird that looked like a needlefish with wings zoomed right in front of his nose. *Did it have two giant front teeth?* If the creature had whizzed by just a second earlier, Tor might have found out.

His stomach did a strange little jump as there was another sharp drop. He found himself in a completely new layer of the jungle.

This part of the rain forest held rows upon rows of stubby, tunnel-shaped plants bunched into bouquets, just like the sun coral back home. As Tor approached an especially large group, the flora closed up, tentacle-like petals hiding away. Then, at the exact moment Tor passed by—

They burst.

One by one, like cannons, they shot fluorescent powder right onto him. He closed his eyes and coughed, wishing he could wipe his face, but knowing the consequences of letting the handle go. By the time he had zipped away from the strange plants, his clothes were covered in dramatic shades. Even his hair was full of the dust, which he tried his best to shake away.

He broke through a final piece of the forest, full of the many glowing plants he had already seen, before the tips of his feet caught roughly on the ground. They dragged for just a few seconds before he let go.

He catapulted forward and landed on his face.

Melda groaned in front of him, still plastered to the ground like an egg in a pan.

"That was awesome!" Engle jumped around them in circles, shooting his arms into the air. He was covered in color, head to toe. They all were, all except for Koso, who must have known a way to keep the plants from shooting out their powder. "Again?"

Melda peeled herself off the dirt long enough to skewer him with a glare.

Koso, meanwhile, looked distracted, squinting into the distance, looking like Engle when he spied something far away. *Could he also be a sightseer?*

Koso broke into a wide grin. "Come now, there's something nearby I want to show you."

Melda was still trying to dust herself off. She had about three types of dirt and mud on her face. "No, no way, nothing else from *you*."

"No more zipping for now, I promise. Just walking."

Tor didn't move an inch, his heart still beating as fast as a hummingbird's wings.

"Come on!"

"Where are we going?"

"A tree has fallen!"

Tor and Melda looked at each other. "So?"

Koso sighed. "Our canopy is so thick that normally only a very limited amount of light shines through." Tor had experienced that much. The treetops were close enough together to allow for a village to have been formed on *top* of them, after all. "So, when a tree falls, it creates what we call a lightstream."

Melda scrunched up her nose. "What's so special about that?"

"You'll see."

They walked through the rain forest in a line, with Koso at the front.

Melda still did not seem satisfied with the explanation. "And how did you know about this *lightstream* when we were standing all the way over there?"

Koso shrugged. "It's part of my emblem."

"Are you a sightseer?" Tor asked.

He shook his head. "No, but I'm very sensitive to moonlight," he explained. "It changes me."

Melda's brow bent in about five different places. "What do you mean the moon *changes* you?"

"When it's full, I transform. Into an animal, mostly, but I've been a plant before, too. One of those flowers that shoots out colored dust, actually—they have better aim than you might think." He winked. "And trust me, they hit you on purpose."

Engle stopped dead in his tracks. He opened and closed

his mouth like a confused fish. Tor had never quite seen him so lost for words. "You're...you're..." He blinked. "You're a *morphite*?"

Koso nodded.

"What's your animal? No, let me guess. An eel. No, a hawk! That's what I'd choose."

He laughed. "I've been both of those. Every new moon is different. Depends on loads of things, I suppose—the weather, my dreams...the number of cocoanuts I've had that day. Soon though, I'll have to choose one."

Engle threw his hands into the air. "Some people have all the luck!" He turned to Tor. "Do you think if we find the Night Witch, I can trade emblems?"

Though Tor knew he wasn't serious, it still triggered something. The fact that Engle could want an emblem other than his own was proof he wasn't the only one who felt unsatisfied with their lot. If Tor really thought about it, Engle's passion had always been for animals—being born with a creature-based emblem *did* seem more fitting than the one he had.

Maybe the wish-gods' science of giving out markings was flawed. And not just for Tor.

Melda rolled her eyes and shook her head, just as she broke through a thick shrub. "Ungrateful, the both of you," she said. Then, she blinked.

Right in front of them appeared a stream of moonlight so thick it looked like fabric—star-woven, just like in the stories. Smooth as silk, and glistening, shooting out of a small hole in the canopy like a finger from the heavens poking through.

And they were not the only ones admiring the light-stream. Animals from all around the rain forest had gathered, standing on the outskirts of the radiance, the sparkling light like a beacon.

Engle rattled off their names in a whisper. "Ram-horned stag, four-fingered sloth, spotted ocelot, tiger butterfly, gato oscuro, willow orangutan, winged slug!"

Tor had never seen so many creatures in one spot. These were species he had only ever heard Engle describe at lunch-time. Seeing them in the flesh, lit up in glowing colors no less, seemed fit for a dream.

Something croaked nearby in a soft tune. A tiny frog, covered in bright blue stripes, just like a tiger's, jumped right onto his arm. He smiled down at it, reaching out a finger to trail down its back.

"Tor, no!" Engle lunged to slap the animal away with a branch, and it jumped before he could, disappearing into a reed shaped like a green tunnel. The creature had only been on Tor's skin for a matter of seconds.

But it was too late.

"My arm...my skin, it's..." Tor screamed out, making more than a few of the animals in front of him turn around. "It's on fire!"

It was as if he had been bitten by a mouthful of flames, his flesh igniting like a match. His lungs felt as though they had been punctured, his throat filled with moss.

He heard pieces of sentences as his friends rushed around him, felt the pierce of a stump in his back as he fell.

"Dart frog—"

"His heart—"

"Not breathing—"

And then the last word he heard, before even the moonlight fell away: "*Deadly.*"

LIFELINES

O nce upon a foaming sea, a woman was born with an emblem never before seen. That of a rainbow circle, right in the middle of her palm. She could sense what time the sun would rise. She knew if the day of hunting would be successful and if her fruit tree would survive the winter. She was a seer, and, once word spread about her abilities, she became very busy.

A line streamed out of her house and down through the village, along the coast, and to the mountains—full of Emblemites wanting to know their fate. As a rule, the woman never gave specifics about one's destiny. Instead, she would provide a broad outline of a person's life.

She would take their hand into her own. Then run her finger across their palms. In the places she touched, rainbow streaks appeared in a pattern that showed the highs and lows of their future.

Emblemites learned to read their lifelines like reading a clock—knowing that the brightest parts represented where they were along their journey.

They guessed at how long they had to live. Some were just happy to know the path their life would take. Others tried so hard to avoid their fate, they forgot to live their lives.

When the seer passed on, she left her emblem's gift behind in pockets of air, in between the stars, and underneath river stones. From that point on, all children were born with their own lifeline, painted across their hands.

Some were grateful for that knowledge.

And others deemed it a curse.

9

THE CRYSTALS

Tor woke up choking. His skin was burning, and sweat soaked his clothes. He was in some sort of hut.

Thump, thump thump. Tor turned to see an old man next to him, wearing a sweeping shawl and grinding something in a small bowl. He smeared the bright blue substance across Tor's forehead; it chilled him to the bone.

"We have to break the fever," the man explained. He held a bright rock in his hand. "It's a healing crystal," he said, noticing Tor's look. He walked to the edge of the hut and opened the door wide. "We have many varieties in Zura."

Outside the room, at the base of several trees, sat clusters of long, pointed crystals.

"Clear-colored for alertness, rose for love, gray for remembering dreams, green for eliminating negativity, purple for renewal, and, of course, bright blue for healing." The old man pursed his thin lips. "Without which you would be very much dead."

Tor nodded, still feeling dazed, like he had awoken from a hundred-year hibernation. "Who are you?" His voice came out as more of a croak.

"They call me a curador." He shrugged. "But I'm just like you. A little older, of course." He laughed. "Okay, perhaps a lot older."

The man wiped his hands on a cloth, and the sight made Tor's eyes widen even more than the crystals had. His palms were not covered by a lifeline, but by winding, silver scars.

"We cut them away, as children," the curador said.

Tor gasped, the movement sending a wave of nausea through him. "You cut your lifeline off? Why?"

The old man moved the blue crystal above Tor's body, from head to toe, then back again. He could feel its energy, a shiver of iciness spreading through him. There was ringing in his ears, the same ringing he always heard underwater.

"We find the idea a bit paralyzing," the curador explained.

Tor did not have to ask the man what he meant. He knew. He had spent years staring at his lifeline, wishing for peaks, or even valleys, just to make his life interesting. He had, in a way, allowed those rainbow lines to control his life. His actions. Tor began to wonder... If he hadn't known what a comfortable future he had in store, would he have risked his emblem for a new one?

Would he have submitted such a foolish wish on Eve?

"When your lifeline is gone, you're free to decide who you want to be," the curador said. He motioned down to Tor's own palm. "Don't you think so?" Before Tor could respond, the old man struck his hands together. A bell rang out sharply through the hut, and the crystal the curador had been holding crumbled into powder.

The moment the rock specks floated down onto his skin, Tor's body rose—floated in the air for just a moment—then fell.

And Tor was in darkness yet again.

He opened his eyes to find Engle and Melda's faces right above his own.

She threw her arms around his neck. "We thought you were a goner!"

Engle nodded, impressed. "Dart frogs are the most poisonous animal on all of Emblem Island," he said. He pursed his lips. "You really *should* be dead." Melda elbowed him in the shoulder. "*Ow.* Not that I'm complaining or anything."

Tor sat up and groaned. Though he couldn't see any,

his entire body might as well have been covered in bruises. Everything hurt. "How long was I out?"

"Almost all night," Engle said. "Enough time for us to have slept a bit, gotten dinner, and, best of all, *drumroll please...* figured out where to go next."

Melda cleared her throat.

"Okay, the curador figured it out, but I showed him the book."

Melda blinked at him.

"Okay, he didn't need the book, Melda told him the pelilarga story, and he figured it out." Engle's face lit up, and he dug into his pocket. "But I *did* get you this!" He produced a handful of crumbs, then frowned. "Oh. Must have...um...fallen apart."

The curador handed Tor a cup of something bright red. Probably ground from crystals. "Drink this. For strength."

He took a sip, and almost spit it out. It tasted like a mixture of sour dirt and mossy bark.

"Vile, but it'll do the trick."

Tor gulped it down in one go, then winced. "So where... where—*emblem*, that's awful." He grimaced. The crystal drink had an even worse aftertaste. "Where are we going next?" Though being poisoned by the dart frog had been the most painful experience of his life, Tor felt a slight rush of relief that his friends had figured out the next step in their journey without him.

Melda laced her hands together. She looked nervous...no, *afraid*. "Perhaps the curador should explain."

The old man squinted, looking down at Tor from where he stood. "I've heard of these beings. The ones from the story your friend told me. There are legends northeast of here, of women with long, wicked hair that they can control like whips. Stories of men disappearing, without a trace. Of echoing screams."

That definitely sounded like the creatures from the fairy tale. "Where?"

"The Scalawag Range."

Hearing that name, that place, made Tor's stomach do all types of terrible things. It sunk because he actually knew of this location, of its treacherous paths and the carnivorous animals that lived there. It also squirmed with shame. Because, for the first time in what seemed like a while, he thought of Rosa.

His little sister... How was she doing? Was she worried about her brother?

"A treacherous journey, no doubt," the curador said. "You'll be needing supplies...yes, yes...perhaps a few crystals to guard against the dark spirits? And food, of course, you won't find even a weed in *those* mountains. Might have to fast a bit, depends on how much you can carry, I suppose." The more he spoke, the more Tor's confidence in their abilities faded.

Koso yawned. Tor hadn't noticed he had walked into the

hut until now. "Talk of imminent death makes me drowsy. We have just a handful of hours left in the night, and I don't know about you, but I plan to spend them with my eyes *closed*."

His yawn was contagious and soon spread across the group, infecting everyone except for the curador. Through the doorway, they watched him pick crystals from the bases of his trees as simply as plucking flowers in a garden. The glowing rocks slipped out of the dirt with ease, their bright color flickering, then returning to their previous glory. Once he had a bushel, the old man looked down at his selection and nodded, satisfied. "This should do. Keep them close by, and make sure—are you listening? This is important. Make *sure* you don't let them touch the ground. Once picked, crystals are never supposed to return to the soil."

Melda squinted. "What happens if they touch the ground?"

The curador shivered. His bald head caught a glimmer of light. "Well, all sorts of things *could* happen. Earthquakes, tornadoes...fire-covered boulders falling from the sky. Or, nothing at all. It all depends on *which* crystal falls, I should say. Some are moodier than others." The curador held one of the long crystals to his chest, a green one, and stroked it the way one might a child. "Every single one has its own flair, and, if we're lucky enough, their tremendous energies are shared with us." He nodded. "Go ahead, take it."

Melda looked like she would rather jump into quicksand, but allowed the curador to place the crystal in her hands. She sighed. "Am I supposed to be feeling something?"

"It's all right, everyone starts somewhere. Close your hand around it. In fact, Tor, Engle, why don't you try it as well?"

They all locked their hands around the emerald-colored rock at once—and it glowed even brighter than before, so brilliantly that Tor had to close his eyes against the flash of light. The crystal began to quiver, trembling beneath their grip.

All at once, like a blast of sunlight melting a clump of dirty snow, all of his worries started to thaw...

Rosa. The guilt he carried for leaving her faded.

The curse. An image of the eye on his wrist made his stomach twist into a braid. Slowly, however, it began to disentangle, as his worries were expelled.

Lastly—

The Night Witch. The thought of her was a massive glacier, fear frozen solid. His chest tightened as pieces of her stories flitted through his mind...

But, unlike every other time before, none of those images stuck. Tor's fear slowly but surely began to defrost, until it softened into a more manageable mound. He was still afraid, of course. But his journey seemed more possible now than it ever had before. Achievable, even.

Tor opened his eyes to find that Melda's constantly tense shoulders had relaxed. The expression she wore reminded him of Rosa waking up from a nap, one foot still stuck in dreamland. She looked odd, he thought, without the worry lines that typically crumpled her forehead into a folded-up fan.

Engle's eyes were still closed, and he swayed gently back and forth like a foamy ocean wave, humming a soothing song.

"Works wonders, doesn't it?" The curador watched them with delight, his hands intertwined in front of him. "Only downside—*side effect*, if you will—is that use of crystals can make one quite drowsy. Then again, it is time to sleep now, isn't it? Koso, why don't you show our guests to their beds?"

Tor stumbled out of the hut after his friends, his limbs so relaxed they could have been softened sticks of butter. The crystal's calming effect made it so that when Koso presented a hammock hanging fifty feet above the rain forest floor as a bed, Tor did not even complain. In fact, he *smiled*.

He fell asleep to the sound of Melda, somewhere near him, joyfully humming herself to sleep.

A sliver of light on Tor's face woke him the next morning. He had only slept a couple of hours, but jumped up at once, filled with energy. Neither the fact that the hammock rocked dangerously to one side—*this* close to flipping over—nor a glimpse of the eye on his arm could bring Tor's spirits down. For the first time since he had been cursed, he felt light as a feather.

He briefly wondered how long it would be before the crystal's effects wore off.

They ate breakfast on the Canopy, miles from the cocoanut hut. This part of the market looked nearly the same, but it had larger structures, including an archway made entirely of flowers. It was early, and most of the stands were still boarded up, but Koso had managed to get them eggs, scooped-out avocado, and a bowl of mashed acai topped with cinnamon and sliced banana. Tor ate quickly, grateful for his first full meal in days.

When even Engle's black hole of a stomach was stuffed, Koso gifted them two bags—one filled with food and water, and the other holding the sack of crystals the curador had given them the night before.

Then, he led them to the zippy, the fastest way out of Zura. And their proximity to the glowing, calming rocks was no doubt the reason why neither Tor nor Melda said a word.

"Farewell," Koso said. "I wish I could say we will see each other again, but, well—no guarantees, right?" He laughed nervously.

His words didn't make Tor feel better, but they didn't exactly make him feel *worse*, either. "Thank you for everything. And we *will* see each other again. That's a promise,"

Tor said, with about ten times the confidence he actually felt, even with the crystal's help. He squeezed the zippy's handle so tightly, his knuckles turned pale.

Koso nodded as Chico shrieked a goodbye. Then, with a final encouraging smile, he bounced heavily on the wooden platform, sending Tor, Melda, and Engle careening down into the rain forest.

The moment they landed and stepped out of Zura, Tor, Melda, and Engle were showered with sunlight so thick and bright, it was as though they were emerging from a cave. Tor covered his eyes with his hand, but the sun's rays found the rest of his body, toasting him in seconds.

"How far until the mountains?" Engle asked, chewing on a fruit from their store.

Melda unfurled the map. "Farther than you'd like." Tor followed her finger across the parchment's colors—across a sea of gold, then blue, then, finally, to a mess of peaks resembling a scaled creature's back.

The Scalawag Range.

Even though they were traveling right toward danger, toward soul-stealing creatures, at least they had a plan.

Tor swallowed, wondering if a bad plan was worse than no plan at all.

MELODINES AND CAPTIVATES

O nce upon a midnight hour, the sea felt it was owed a debt. Over time, ships had become sturdier, so sound that sailors often traveled upon the ocean's back without a drop of blood as payment.

That will not do, the sea said. So, from its depths, it created a creature that would balance the scales of life and death.

With skin as glittering as sea foam, hair silkier than water, eyes the purple of sea glass, and a voice more alluring than the sound of curling waves, the first melodine was born.

When the next ship sailed by, the water around it began to swirl in miniature whirlpools. It glittered with the dazzle of the nighttime sky, like a pirate had tipped his treasure right into the ocean, and left a trail of gemstones in his wake. The anchor heaved over the side, and sailors leaned over the edges of the ship for a look, just as a head peeked through the water. That of a woman.

Then, another head. That of a man.

Their eyes broke through the night like beams of light. The sailors were hypnotized, falling from the deck, one after the other, without the melodines even opening their mouths.

Over time, stories were passed down and sailors became wary. Now they know better than to look too closely at the waves. They keep their eyes on the horizon and stuff their ears with beeswax when the sun sets. So the melodines traveled to distant waters—ponds, streams, and rivers began to shimmer with their magic as they awaited their next meal. The water they inhabited became a black hole of hunger. A trap.

A captivate.

Beware a lake that does not run clear. Beware the whispers of bubbles in your ear. Beware flower petals in water that seep color. For you might have found yourself in a captivate. And sheer willpower is the only escape.

10

THE GOLDEN OCEAN

They traveled for hours in a heat so thick Tor swore it had its own color. Like a fog, the humidity surrounded them and weighed down their limbs, making even walking a grueling task.

Tor did not think it could get worse, until it did.

The soft grass of the plains beyond the rain forest soon became sand. Yellow dunes stretched as far as they could see, waves of gold that looked much prettier than they felt underneath their feet.

"It's a desert," Melda said, reaching down and taking some of the sand into her hand.

Tor had seen a painting of a desert once, but looking at a picture of one and actually trudging through one were two very different things. The streak of yellow on the map suddenly made sense. "We'll have to be very careful to keep straight," he said, knowing that if they veered off their path by just a few degrees, they could find themselves lost in the golden sea for far longer than they could afford. He pulled his gifted dagger from his pocket, its metal cool in his hand. He would use it to draw a line through the dunes, he decided, to help keep them from swerving too far in the wrong direction.

Despite the heat, Tor almost enjoyed the whisper of sand blowing through the wind around him; he liked the way his shoes sunk down into the ground, cushioning each step.

But then the thirst came. Everything was so dry—burnt, in a way. He found himself wondering if perhaps this endless stretch of sand used to be a different color but had eventually been scorched into the same shade as the sun.

The landscape never changed. There were no new flowers to let them know that they had made progress. No animals to entertain them with their songs. It was as if they had walked the same stretch of land for hours.

Tor's mouth became a bowl of dust, barren, his tongue a dried-up sponge.

"Not yet," Melda whispered when the boys asked for the canteens, knowing there was still a long way ahead of them. It was her turn holding the backpack.

So Tor daydreamed of water instead, thinking of its pure

flavor, the texture he had never appreciated until now. Its silky, slithery dance down his throat. He imagined waterfalls in his mind and thought about how incredible it would be to stand beneath one. He pictured what the beaches at home looked like, thinking to himself how unnatural sand was in this much quantity.

When he reached for the fruits they had been gifted in Zura, he found they had dried up into cores, the desert having sucked the life right out of them.

Hours felt like their own lifetimes, each step becoming harder and harder. When Engle fell to his knees, Tor could not find the strength to help him up—he had sweat all of his energy away. He felt as useless as the dried-up fruit. So, he fell down, too. Melda made it a few more steps, then collapsed. She fished for the water and gave it to the boys, but even that was not enough. Tor blinked once, twice, then one last time, before his body seemed to give up.

Tor gasped, inhaling sand as he did. He doubled over and coughed, a cloud of dust expelling from his mouth.

The sun was gone. A moon sat in its place, its pale face a welcome sight. The air was noticeably cooler, the sand softer.

A thin sheet of it covered his body, almost as if the desert had given him a blanket.

He stood and walked over to Melda. "Wake up," he whispered. She did not move. "Wake up," he said louder and tapped her on the shoulder.

She awoke, and Tor had never been so happy to see the blue of her eyes. Then, she scowled. "I feel like I already died." Her voice sounded much raspier than usual.

He helped her up. "Me too."

Tor woke Engle, whose own eyes looked painfully red. "I can hardly see a thing," he said, which Tor found ironic. A sightseer's eyes, however, were known to be much more delicate than others, given that they worked so much harder.

Trying not to think too much about the scratch of his throat, Tor dragged his feet against the sand, creating two rough lines. The trail left behind them by the dagger was long gone, swept away by the same sand and wind that had covered him where he'd fallen. Though they had rested for hours, it seemed about time for another nap...

Melda swallowed, the sound rough and dry. "Guys? I don't think we're walking in the right direction." Her teeth knocked together. "I don't even know what the right direction is anymore." Melda, as usual, was right.

Tor tried to look more confident than he felt. "Let's just

keep moving." But doubts filled his brain. If they really *were* moving in the wrong direction, they could very well die of dehydration before reaching another village. According to the map, the desert spanned dozens of miles.

"Can you see anything now?" Tor asked Engle. If he could zoom his vision, he might be able to tell them where to go.

His friend rubbed his eyes and blinked about a dozen times. He squinted, turned in a circle, then winced. "No," he said. "All I see is hazy yellow."

"It's all right," Tor said. "We'll find our way."

A few moments later, Melda broke into a coughing fit, doubling over. Puffs of powder came out of her mouth, like sand had been ground into her lungs. Engle continued to scrub his eyes to no avail and eventually had to lean against Tor, following his direction, blinded.

This would be a terrible way to die, Tor thought. He didn't want to be buried in a desert for eternity. He supposed they were likely walking over bones right now...

No, he would not give up. He locked arms with Melda and pulled Engle closer to his side, then pushed farther, his friends stumbling next to him. This was *his* fault; they were here because of *his* wish.

It was up to him to get them out. He wouldn't give up until he dropped dead.

Something echoed across the dunes.

It was the long screech of a bird. Loud, like it was sitting right on Tor's shoulder. His first reaction was to wonder if it was real—or possibly a mirage.

Then, the screeching got louder.

Engle squinted at the sky. "What is it?" he asked.

Tor's lips parted to answer, but nothing came out. Something just as silver as the moon flew overhead. Its feathers glowed through the darkness.

Melda stopped walking altogether. "It can't be," she said.

Tor blinked, waiting for the bird to disappear. But it didn't, instead flying in circles right above where they stood.

"Well, what is it?" Engle asked.

"It looks like a silver falcon."

Engle's bloodshot eyes flew open. "A silver *what*?"

Tor was still watching the bird, a bird that shouldn't exist— the mystical messenger of the wish-gods. After a few more circles, it started to fly away. "I think it wants us to follow."

A fire of excitement lit up in his belly. The silver falcon was helping them—which only meant one thing.

Tor really was on a Grail.

The three of them took off after the spectacular bird, its silver wings cutting right through the night sky like metallic scissors. They did not travel feet, or even yards, but miles.

Miles of moving without food or water for fuel, of periodically closing their eyes against the sand and then staring up at the falcon, using it as a guiding star.

They ran though their limbs ached; they gasped for air when their lungs threatened to burst; they kept moving though they thought their bones might simply break.

By the time the silver falcon finally slowed down, they were golden all over, a layer of sand coating their clothing—Melda's dark hair was full of it. The small grains looked like salt.

Then, the creature stopped, still beating its giant wings, body fixed in place. It screeched happily, the sound like a cheer. When they were directly beneath the bird, they came to a stop, too. Tor swallowed.

There, in front of them, was a most welcomed color.

Green.

"An oasis," Melda said.

And blue.

A long stream flowed before them, framed by rows of plants, impossibly tall flowers that stood hunched over, and miniature trees that held tiny fruits. By the time Tor lifted his head to thank the bird, it had flown away.

Water—finally. Tor wanted to jump inside and never have a need to surface.

Engle picked a yellow fruit from one of the tiny, waist-high trees shaped like mushrooms. He took a bite and closed his eyes, its juices dripping down his chin, leaving streaks on his dusty face. Tor and Melda did not even stop to try one. Their eyes were fixed on the ribbon of water before them.

Tor took a trembling step forward, the lake pulling at him like they were tied together by yarn. His heart raced, his skin tingled, his toes curled.

And, without wasting another moment, he jumped in.

When Tor plunged into the stream, the sand washed free from his clothing, hair, and eyelashes. It even carried away the leftover plant powder color from his outfit. The water cooled his slightly pinked skin, healing it from the sun's fury just as streams of bubbles exploded out of his nostrils.

It was much deeper than Tor had imagined. He sank until he felt like his organs might implode, and still did not reach the bottom. When he emerged, he savored the moment, eyes closed. Both body and mind were revitalized, revived, by the sleek, cool rush of water.

He opened his eyes.

The pool had burst into a thousand different shades. Ripples of lavender, indigo, rose, emerald, and gold spiraled away from their movements, sparkling. The water flowed as if it were alive, dancing across the surface. A kaleidoscope come to life, it was mesmerizing. Hypnotizing.

Tor drank the liquid, unable to help himself, and found it was deliciously fruity. Its flavor reminded him of the special tea his father made in the summer, infused with blueberries and fig. He cupped more in his hand and watched the confetti of color swirl in his palm. Tor drank it, then had some more, his thirst insatiable. Suddenly, the thought of drinking any other type of liquid seemed unbearable. Nothing compared to this.

Melda floated on her back, the water outlining her body in a vibrant purple. For just a moment, she looked relaxed.

Tor watched as she ducked her head underwater, her hair and ribbons creating a halo around her head as she swam to the other side.

"Okay, I think it's time to go," she was saying as she filled their canteens. He didn't move. "Engle? Tor?"

Tor refused to look away from the water.

"Hello?" she said. Then, she said it louder.

But he didn't want to answer. *Couldn't* answer. It was as if his lips had melted together. He felt so drowsy, so heavy. Like a boulder about to sink to the bottom of a river...

"Engle?" Melda screamed.

"Come back in! It's delicious," Engle said, throwing his hands up over his head. "Delicious as a dream."

"We don't have time. Please just get Tor—"

"No," Engle replied, matter-of-factly. "I think I'll stay. I think I'll stay forever."

There was silence.

"It's a captivate!" Melda screamed.

Tor felt someone hook a finger through his shirt. *Engle.* His friend started dragging him across the water, toward where Melda stood. But the closer they got to shore, the more Tor struggled, kicking and yelling.

"We're in a captivate," Engle told him, but the word did nothing to calm him. He fought to stay inside, attempting to dive deeper into the lake.

He didn't want to leave. What could be better than this? He had always wanted to live in water, far away from school and the village's rules. He could stay here, in the stream, swim every day and never have to go home...

Engle pulled harder, and suddenly, the water lurched in the opposite direction, taking Tor with it. The pool was trying to keep him. And he didn't mind one bit.

"He has to leave of his own volition," Melda said, helping Engle back onto land.

They screamed Tor's name, and he heard them, but his

eyes were glued to the water, its shades swirling faster now, colors erupting every second—a fireworks show just for him. Then came the singing.

Dozens of voices like strings of a harp, perfectly pitched and effortless, silk draped against silk.

"Oh no," Engle said.

Thin tails peeked out of the water, then unfurled into fans. The creatures circled around and around Tor, creating a whirlpool. He was their dinner. Somewhere in the corner of his mind he knew that, but he continued to smile, enraptured.

"Do something!" Melda said, in a panic.

But there was not much they *could* do. Victims of captivates could only escape of their own free will. Tor could not be forced, but he could be convinced.

And no one knew him better than Engle did.

"Think about Estrelle!" he yelled. "You want to go back home, right?" Tor remained transfixed, his village far from his mind. "Remember the twinetrees, and your dad's nutmeg bread! The cherry-berry ice pops! The emerald cream!" Tor didn't move an inch.

"It's not working," Melda said, her voice shaking. They had all read about captivates and their melodines in *Cuentos*.

The beautiful creatures poked their heads up, their violet eyes shining as brightly as freshly cut gems. Their rose-colored lips mouthed the sweetest of songs. All that was left was for them to reveal their sharklike teeth...

"Remember Rosa!" Engle screamed. At the mention of his sister's name, Tor turned his head. *Rosa.* He could almost see her lifeline in his mind...

The sea creatures continued to swim and swim around him, desperate.

"Remember Rosa," Engle repeated.

Tor blinked.

"Her voice is far better than theirs."

All at once, the spell was broken. Tor groaned.

The stream fell still. Colors disappeared. The music was gone, captured. And Tor, forehead crinkled as if awaking from a bad dream, floated through the waters, toward Melda's outstretched arms.

THE PELILARGAS

Once upon a dark kingdom, there was a ruler who longed to marry a woman with long, beautiful hair. "I shall fill her locks with my treasures, to keep them safe," he declared.

The town crier announced this news to the townsfolk.

In response, a maiden inquired: "Is he kind?"

"He's a *king*, madam," the crier responded, shocked at her question.

She blinked back at him. "I asked if he is *kind*," she repeated.

"Of course," he replied. "He is a good man. A man of honor and a fair ruler."

At that, several women instructed their hair to grow, eager to meet such a king. Five springs passed, and the women arrived at the palace at last, hair so long their sisters walked behind them, carrying the rest of their locks in baskets.

But the king was not the man that had been promised. One look at his suitors and he declared, "I cannot decide. No matter—I have enough treasure to take all of you as my brides."

Their hair began to be filled with gems of every shade: diamonds, rubies, emeralds, sapphires, pearls, and jade. And the women realized they had been deceived—for this king was not kind, just, or good.

"When it is dark, we will run away, and take the fool's treasure with us," one of the women told the others. And they agreed it was a good plan.

That night, the women fled—not only the castle, but the kingdom, afraid of being caught by the king's army. They escaped into a jungle, hair wrapped around themselves to keep the gems in place.

Angry at the deception and pleased with the robbery, the women decided they did not wish to stop. They went from village to village, stealing treasure from foolish men.

They stole until their hair was heavy with jewels. More than enough to buy their own palace, far away from the king they once knew. But they wanted more. The gems had seeped into not only their hair, but their minds, filling them with an insatiable greed.

The women's power grew and soon they could steal more than treasure—they were able to steal a person's soul. They first targeted a group known for harming the jungle they often inhabited. Next, a man who had betrayed his entire family for power. The more tainted, the better.

Souls made their hair grow longer and stronger. Made them more powerful than gems ever had. They retreated into the mountains, leaving a trail of glittering stones as bait for unsuspecting travelers.

So the first pelilargas came to be.

Beware their hair, which they use not for holding treasure—but as weapons. And do not stare into their rotting eyes, two charcoal holes. For they see the darkest parts of a heart, before piercing through a soul.

11

THE SCALAWAG RANGE

When the sand turned to rock and the horizon was blocked by a monstrous mountain range, the moon still hung in the sky like a giant pearl.

Finally, Melda spoke. "You skipped the story, didn't you?" she said, quiet enough that Engle, who was a few steps ahead, didn't hear.

He nodded, not meeting her eyes.

"Why?"

"I read the first part, I just thought—I thought it would save us time to skip to the next one." He had forgotten the end. If he had read the part about the captivate, he would have been warier of the oasis.

"There are no shortcuts," she said. "You said that. You said we have to follow the monster myths perfectly." She looked over at him, and Tor looked away. He knew he had messed up. She shook her head. "It's my fault, too. I should have realized we missed a story."

As much as he wished she hadn't brought it up, Melda was right. He needed to be more careful. Things were only going to get harder.

They should be sleeping, Tor thought, yet he didn't feel tired. They had slept the day away in the desert, after all. And there was no time to waste. So even though Tor was sure the pelilargas were more frightening in the dark, they continued forward.

"What do we do if we see them?" Engle asked. He held their light bulb in his palm, the small ball looking like a magical orb. "Do I throw this at them?"

Melda sighed heavily. "Yes, please do rid us of our only source of light. And by *us* I mean the two people who don't have the ability to see in the dark." She grabbed the orb from his hand. "You don't even need this."

"Hey!" Engle said. "I like holding it."

Tor wondered if he should get the calming green crystal out again...for more than a few reasons. A small spark of panic had lit in his stomach, and he worried it might burst into a fire of anxiety. What *would* they do if the pelilargas came out of hiding? Throwing a ball of light surely wouldn't stop one of those creatures, let alone dozens.

"We run," he said simply. "We don't look them in the eyes, just like the story says, and we run."

They started up a hill covered in soft dirt, one that, according to the map, led to the main passage through the mountains. The Scalawag Range covered several miles of land in all directions and was only passable on a single trail that stretched across its very top—one that was famously narrow and ran up and down in rough, jagged swells resembling stormy ocean waves. Its narrow path often led to travelers falling hundreds of feet off its sides.

As bad as that sounded, however, taking any other way was worse. Engle often spoke of the terrible, carnivorous animals that called the base of the mountain home, waiting like hungry sharks to tear up whatever fell from its peak.

No, going across the mountain range's summit was the only way.

Melda stopped so suddenly, Tor almost ran right into her back.

In front of them stood a door, rooted into the ground like a tree.

"What's a door doing here?" Engle asked, scratching his head. "Do you think it's been enchanted by a telecorp to take us directly to the other side of the mountain range?"

Melda glared at him. "If we were that lucky, then we

wouldn't have this curse in the first place." She reached out and yanked open the odd door.

She had one leg in the air, about to take a step through the opening, when she stopped. Just beyond the threshold, the passageway narrowed to three feet wide. A path like a tight-rope. One step in either direction and she would have surely tumbled right off the cliff.

For miles and miles, there was just the slender, snake-like road, with deathly drops on either side. "I suppose this is the entrance," she said quietly.

"Looks like it," Tor replied, before following her through the door.

● ☽ ☽ ☾

Tor kept his eyes on his feet. Though there was just enough room for him to walk normally, he chose to place one foot directly in front of the other. One wrong step could send him plummeting. The higher they climbed, the stronger the wind became, roaring in Tor's ears, whipping at his cheeks. He steadied himself against it, hoping the current wouldn't tip him to one side.

Melda was in front, slowing the line down, but for once Tor was grateful for her slug-like pace.

"Gets a bit thicker farther down," Engle said from somewhere behind him, referring to the path. "There are a few ledges up ahead, too." Tor realized Engle should probably be leading the way, given his emblem. But it was too late to switch the order now.

The light bulb's illumination reached just far enough for Tor to be able to see where he was going. His stomach dropped as he imagined for about the tenth time what would happen if his balance failed him—this time, in particular, he pictured being cut to ribbons by the slope's rocky exterior, before landing in the center of a pack of wolves.

A shiver slithered down his spine.

Stop it. He tried to think of something a little more positive.

At least the pelilargas had yet to make an appearance. That was a plus. Maybe they *weren't* nocturnal, like he figured, and were fast asleep. Maybe Tor, Engle, and Melda wouldn't see them at all, would just make their way across the mountain range without any trouble...

He sighed. Melda was right. They didn't have that sort of luck.

"Should we start thinking about our next stop?" she said from up ahead.

"All right." It seemed like at least a small distraction from the silence that had blanketed their path, interrupted only by the wind, the same type of quiet he might have expected from sailing in the middle of the ocean—nothing else for miles.

Or, at least, nothing else *yet.*

He didn't need to get the book from his backpack to know which tale came next. "This next one is the easiest. We're clearly going to Frostflake," Tor said, referencing the town in "The Snowbeast." "Wherever that is. How about the one after that?"

"That's the one with the giant, right?" Engle said.

"Not just a giant, a *giantess*, too. It's called 'The Giantess Nar.' This one's my favorite. I know where to go!" Melda yelled enthusiastically, her voice echoing through the night.

Before she could say another word, the ground began to shake.

Tor lost his footing, tumbled to the side—and would have fallen hundreds of feet if it wasn't for Engle's fast reflexes. Melda was on her hands and knees, gripping the rock tightly. She looked over her shoulder, fear twisting her face. "They're here," she said.

Tor looked over the edge and gulped.

Women wrapped in dark hair crawled out of caves dug into the mountain's slope. With long, curved nails, they climbed the side like manic animals, emitting high-pitched screams on their way.

"Run!" Engle yelled. But that was easier said than done. The ground still shook, crumbling the edges of the path, making their trail smaller and smaller.

They ran as fast as they could, arms out to their sides like walking on string, swaying with every step. Tor's ankles twisted painfully as the mountain moved beneath him like a wild beast, and his stomach lurched every few feet, but he kept his eyes on a clearing a few yards ahead, where the narrow path widened. There, at least the ground wasn't ready to give way.

All he had to do was get a little farther...

Melda screamed as she tripped over a large rock, landing right on her stomach. Tor skidded to a halt, arms pinwheeling, and inched toward her carefully, holding out a hand to help her up.

She took it—

But when she pressed her other palm against the ground it fell away completely, taking her down with it.

"No!" Engle yelled.

But Melda wasn't gone yet. Tor hadn't let go of his grip, but the real reason she was still alive was because she had landed on one of the pelilargas' heads, the creature's nails clawed deep into the rock.

Engle lunged to help Tor pull Melda back, and she

screamed as the pelilarga reached up and clawed her ankle, leaving five long, bloody scratches.

"We have you, don't worry," Tor told her, before Melda jerked back. The pelilarga had latched on to her shoe and was tugging her down toward the abyss.

"I'm already gone, go," Melda said, teeth gritted. The pelilarga hissed, and Melda winced, like it had scratched her again. "Take the drop of color, please. And tell my brothers—"

Before she could finish, Engle grunted, pulling with all of his might, and Melda flopped back onto the path. The pelilarga lost its grip and plummeted down into the darkness with a final shriek.

Melda stared at Engle, wide-eyed. Surprised.

"Let's go!" Tor yelled. Other pelilargas had made it onto the passageway. And they were right behind them.

They ran, Melda limping slightly, toward the clearing. But the creatures were there, too, waiting.

They were surrounded.

Black hair like wisps of smoke wrapped around their bodies, the ends curling and uncurling, alive. One of the pelilargas stepped forward. Her face was covered, but her locks had started to part, revealing just the tip of a rotting nose...

"Don't look at her eyes!" Engle yelled. Tor brought his

gaze to the woman's feet, which he watched walk closer and closer, until they were almost directly in front of him.

If he did nothing, they would surely die. The pelilarga would rip them open like candy wrappers then steal their souls. Tor knew that. So he did something risky, absurd—foolish.

He reached into the backpack, grabbed the sack of crystals, and hurled them all to the ground.

The moment the crystals landed, they popped like firecrackers.

One set off an inferno ten feet tall, a wall of flames that grew and expanded faster than water spilling out of a broken vase. It swamped the pelilargas, silencing their hissing screams.

Another crystal turned into a small tornado that toppled off the side of the cliff. A second later, the twister shot up to the sky, suddenly taller than the mountain range.

Tor felt himself starting to lift off the ground, the tornado's winds like a hand sucking him into the stars. Perhaps they wouldn't die at the pelilargas' claws, but being ripped to shreds in a twister didn't seem like a better option at all.

The third crystal trembled on the ground manically, then burst with the suddenness of a kernel of corn popping, turning into what looked like a small ball of cotton. Once it grew, it took the shape of a cloud. Water shot out of it in a wide stream, then hardened into sheets of ice that kept growing and growing, longer and longer still, until its frozen wake dripped down the mountainside in a sweeping arch to the ground.

Engle, who was gripping a boulder for dear life, reached a hand to Melda, who grabbed Tor before he could be carried away. And gravity yanked him free from the tornado's winds as he plunged down the slide.

THE SNOWBEAST

Once upon a summer day, a child prayed to the moon for snow. The next morning, she awoke with a ball of ice in her hands and a voice in her ear. *Bury it beneath the largest tree in the town square*, it said.

She did. And the moment the ice found the earth, the tree changed from green to white—feathers replacing its leaves. The clouds above turned silver and released sheets of snowflakes. Villagers gathered outside, faces to the sky, catching the frost on their noses and in their palms.

But this was no ordinary snow. The girl who had wished for the change in weather had a maker's emblem—and she had unknowingly enchanted the ball of ice. Anything created from the snow came to life. Snowmen walked among the villagers. Children rode around on ice horses. Soon, word spread about the strange town of Frostflake.

It was not long before darkness came to claim this magic, for happiness and malice always seem to coexist.

The Night Witch visited this village and stole

almost all of its magical snow, from which she spun a dreadful creature. It climbed toward Frostflake, its shadow longer than the town itself.

Screaming in horror as the beast drew closer, villagers fled into their homes. The child stayed outside and had a thought for how to help. With her friends, she lit dozens of torches, then dug them into the ground surrounding the town. And when the snowbeast arrived, it did not pass, afraid of even the smallest flame. Without a way in, the creature turned around and retreated back into the forest.

There it sits, awaiting the day the torches blow out.

1 2

THE VILLAGE OF
FROSTFLAKE

The slide ended ten feet above the ground, and they landed in a pile of half-melted snow—all that was left of the cloud. Tor flinched as he watched a large bolt of lightning zigzag across the sky, no doubt formed by one of the other crystals.

The curador had been right about several things, one of them being that the use of crystals had made them very tired. Still wet from the snow, they walked until they were dry and reached a small clearing filled with stones large enough to use as beds. After examining their many scratches and sore muscles, they fell asleep, storms still circling the Scalawag Range.

Melda had the map in front of her when Tor woke up.

"We saved a lot of time," she said. "That slide dropped

us off close. Really close." She had her finger pressed against the tiny word Frostflake. "Lucky we don't have to go through *that* stupid place," she said, motioning toward the Plains, which was the exact opposite of stupid, a city home to the best libraries and scholars on the island. It was known for having a highly competitive school, one that only accepted the best student from each emblem. Melda sounded bitter.

Tor woke Engle, and barely an hour passed before they came upon a ring of torches.

He stopped. Beyond the fiery gates was a village white as bone, carved completely from ice. A single silver-tipped cloud hung above it, raining down snow in delicate sweeps. It looked like someone had cut a piece of another universe and placed it there, in the middle of nowhere—a snow globe without its glass.

Melda shivered. "I'm already freezing, best not linger."

They walked between the torches and into the village square. The people of Frostflake wore thick white coats and pants, trimmed in light blue, lined in fleece. And though Tor, Melda, and Engle stuck out in their colored wardrobe, the villagers nodded cheerfully as they passed.

"Creepy, isn't it?" Engle said, pointing toward the ice statues lining the main street. A princess in a sweeping dress. A reindeer. An old man kneeling over a cauldron. "I heard they come to life each night. There're loads of animals you can't find anywhere else here, since the townspeople create them from snow." Engle looked like he wanted to make one of his own—something that could join them on their journey.

Or perhaps something he could eat.

They passed stores that looked like houses selling sugar-coated pastries, gingerbread, and diamond-dusted cider. A woman holding a silver tray of mugs sang a song Tor had never heard before. Something about an enchanted pine branch. She stopped when she spotted Melda, map opened in front of her reddening nose like a newspaper. "Here, have some, you look like you'll soon join the statues!" she said, handing Melda a mug of something emitting a swirl of steam.

Engle looked at the woman expectantly and she handed him, then Tor, a drink as well.

He took a sip, and the liquid was thick as honey, sweet as sapphire; it warmed his throat and settled down into the center of his chest.

"This is lightning!" Engle said, his drink already gone. His eyes went wide when the woman offered him another mug.

"I'm going into the bookshop," Melda said. "We're closer to the Shadows now. They might have something useful."

Tor doubted a cheerful village like this one kept books

about death and Night Witches in stock. Still, he nodded. "We'll wait at the gates."

Before he could reach them, a little girl stepped in his path. Blond braids came out of a hat that looked like an upside-down teacup. "You look cold," she said, mittens coming together. She was about Rosa's age, Tor realized with a pang of sadness.

"We are," Engle said from behind him, his freckles especially visible against his now-pink cheeks.

She crouched down and began smoothing the snow with one of her mittens like painting a canvas, until she had a large rectangle. Then, with a flick of her wrists, she peeled what looked like a sheet of ice from the ground. She shook it the way Tor's mother had taught him to open his sheets, and the frost softened into a blanket. It was made of thick fabric with blue edges.

"Here you go," she said, leaving them with the blanket of snow, then skipping away.

Engle tossed the blanket at Tor, who quickly wrapped it around his shoulders. "I wonder how many things I can make before Melda gets back," he said excitedly, jogging away.

Tor followed him to the edge of town, where the most snow sat, piled in small hills. Maybe they had time to make a few more weapons from the enchanted snow, Tor thought, though he had no idea how long it would take for his creations to harden into something real. The little girl was an expert and likely had an emblem that made creating easier. He sat on the ground and began crafting his best take on a sword.

He quickly recognized the skill that had gone into making his blanket. The snow was lifeless in his hands, falling apart like crumbled pastries. A few failed attempts later, he realized he had to compact the frost in the middle of his palm to make it stick together, which quickly froze his fingers. Still, he kept working. When he was done, the hilt looked a bit lopsided, and the blade might have been too stubby, but it would do. He shrugged, leaving the snow to transform, and tried his hand at a shield.

"Ow." The force of a snowball against his cheek sent him a few inches back. He looked up to see Engle standing there, grinning.

Tor didn't waste a moment before making his own snowball and sending it toward Engle as hard as he could. His friend dodged it at the last moment, then bent down to make another, then another. Engle then combined the two, forming one massive chunk of snow. Tor started to run, laughing, zigzagging. When Engle finally sent it flying, he ducked, and the giant snowball flew right over his head.

Hitting one of the torches instead.

It fell over onto another. And that one also fell, knocking over its neighbor. Tor and Engle watched in silence as the torches tumbled, one by one like dominoes, until the very last light burned out in a hiss against the snow.

There was just a second before the first scream.

A handful of trees trembled slightly, their leaves shaking almost gently. Then a few more—less gently this time. Finally, the entire forest shook.

"Fire! Make a fire!"

"Gather wood!"

"Quickly!"

Tor and Engle rushed back into the village, where chaos had transformed cheerful Frostflake into madness. A man was bent over a pile of branches, desperately rubbing two black stones together. He moved with urgency, but the falling snow made building a fire difficult. After a minute, he produced only a single spark.

"Does anyone have an elemental emblem?" Tor yelled. No one replied. He looked around for the little girl. Could she somehow make flames from the snow?

Melda came rushing out of one of the shops. She locked eyes with Tor. "What on Emblem did you do?"

Tor winced as something snapped in the distance. A tree cut clean in half.

"It's coming!" someone yelled.

The man with the stones worked even faster. He made a flame, but it quickly burnt out against the damp wood.

An old woman had two more rocks and was trying the same thing without much luck.

"Let me see the backpack," Melda said, and Engle handed it to her. She rummaged around for a few moments before her hand surfaced, holding the orb of light. Without missing a beat, she set the orb on the ground, grabbed one of the torches, and used it to smash the glass to pieces.

As soon as the orb broke, its light released in a burst of flames. She dipped the torch inside and held it high over her head, standing beneath the front gate.

There was a moment of silence.

Then, the forest went still.

Sighs of relief were followed by villagers hurriedly using Melda's torch to light the ring of fire once more. They worked quickly, everyone pitching in before the beast decided to attack the village from a different angle. A few people began murmuring, wondering how the flames had possibly gone out in the first place.

Tor, Melda, and Engle slipped out of town as silently as a falling snowflake.

THE GIANTESS NAR

Once upon a burst of light, the sky transformed. When the universe was born, it yawned and screamed—each cry creating its own planet. So beautiful were these little worlds, filled with color and people, they required someone to guard their treasure.

They required a protector.

So, a man taller than the trees and stronger than the seas was formed, his job to guard all creatures from danger. When it rained, the giant gathered the clouds and stroked them until they calmed down. When a tornado appeared, he held it in his hand and squeezed tightly, until it was no more than sand.

He lived for years in isolation, on the peak of a mountain, high enough for him to reach into the sky should he have to shake the sun awake or keep his people dry. The giant lived peacefully in this manner, until one day a traveler happened upon his domain and a hunger awoke. As soon as the giant saw him, he wondered just how good he might taste.

Before he knew it, the deed was done, and he had liked it.

So guardian became huntsman.

Down from his mountain he climbed, throwing into his mouth all the creatures he could find. And though he ate hundreds, his hunger never seemed satisfied.

Word spread of the terrible beast, who had come from the heavens and made the world his feast. The people prayed to the wish-gods, hoping for aid.

"Give us a new protector, one that will not hurt us," they said.

And so, the sky sent a new kind of guardian.

This time, it was a woman. Bigger, stronger, and pure of heart, she defeated the monster and helped make the world new.

She is Nar: the protector of people, sent from the stars.

13

THE RING

"I leave for a few moments, and you two awaken an ancient snowbeast," Melda said, using a ribbon to tie back all of her hair.

The farther from Frostflake they walked, the warmer it became. Once they were out of the shade of huddled clouds, the sun shined down upon them, and the blanket across Tor's shoulders fell to the ground in a puddle. He supposed his shield and sword would have met the same fate, should he have remembered to bring them.

Engle opened his mouth to reply to Melda, and Tor expected a snarky response. But instead, he said, "That was... really quick thinking back there, Melda."

She blinked. Her lips parted, then closed. They continued in silence, Melda walking a little straighter.

A meadow of fat dandelions stretched out to the horizon, fluffy white balls that looked light as air and soft as a sweater. The tickling sensation on Tor's ankles almost made him smile.

Melda looked over her shoulder at them, shrugged, then started running, arms stretched out. As her legs made contact with the flowers, they burst, sending a confetti of white florets flying through the air behind her.

Engle and Tor didn't hesitate in joining in.

They ran and ran, laughing on their way, Tor watching the little pieces of flower floating through the air like little parachutes. They got stuck in Melda's long black ponytail and brushed across Tor's nose.

Engle rolled around the ground. "It smells like summer," he declared. And Tor didn't know what that meant...but somehow it made sense. *He* thought it smelled like the soap his neighbor sold at Estrelle's market every weekend, large lavender-colored bars with flowers trapped inside. When Engle stood up again, white was stuck to his clothes in patches, making him look like a partially plucked chicken.

Tor was just about to laugh, when he heard something. Just a whisper of sound...a sharp zing.

Engle's eyes widened—but, before he could speak a word, Tor winced and reached for his ear.

His fingers came back covered in blood. The tiniest part of his ear, at the very tip, had been cut away.

"Get down!" Engle yelled, spotting something miles off. They immediately sunk to the ground, and Tor heard the same whizzing noise from before, over and over again, quick as rain.

Finally, the whistling stopped.

When Tor looked up, he saw he had been outlined in arrows, the weapons' long points stuck firmly into the ground. Some had landed less than an inch from his body.

Whoever had shot at them had not missed by accident.

They stood, legs trembling, hands raised high over their heads in surrender. And all Tor could do was watch as four figures approached on horseback, bows and arrows still drawn.

As their attackers drew closer, Tor saw that the people on horseback were all women about twice his age, their brown braids decorated with ribbons like Melda's. Their arms were covered from wrist to shoulder in bands of paint, the shades like smeared moonlight against their dark skin.

They did not speak. One of the women jumped off her horse and approached them, strings of rope in hand. As she got closer, Tor could see how tall she really was.

"You're a giantess," Melda said, her voice full of excitement, even though the same woman she was in awe of was currently binding her hands tightly with the rope. The corners of the woman's mouth formed a small smile for just a moment before she turned toward Tor and Engle and tied up them, too. Then, they were each hauled onto the monstrous horses.

Giantesses were said to be the descendants of Nar, the woman giant sent from the stars to protect humans. Over time, according to lore, her descendants had grown smaller and smaller. Now, they stood just over two feet taller than the average Emblemite.

Tor's fingers dug into his palms as they rode, the speed of the horse's galloping making him nauseous. Soon, he caught sight of something up ahead—two rows of torches, holding cups of fire. The women rode between the line of lights, which stretched for a mile and eventually led to a sprawling village.

It was entirely made up of rounded huts like mounds. The doors looked much larger than normal ones—for obvious reasons—and several people walked about, holding weapons that made Tor nervous. One woman polished a sword the size of his entire body. Another wielded a staff, twirling it expertly in her hands.

They passed a market that seemed to sell more weapons than food, metal glinting like diamonds, and the horses did not stop until reaching a hut larger than all of the others, with a symbol painted on the outside. An emblem Tor didn't recognize.

Hands still bound behind them, they were led inside. Tor figured he should be afraid, but something about the giant-esses, as muscular and strong as they clearly were, was gentle.

The hut was simple, without any type of decoration other than a hearth, which burned not wood, but white moss. The flames that flickered were strange, too, tipped with an icy blue Tor had never seen before.

"Burning white makes blue," a woman said. She sat in front of the fire and looked just like the others—long hair in a braid, markings on her arms—yet, there was one difference. She wore a thin band around her head right below a plunging widow's peak, almost like a crown. "Burning purple makes red. Green makes orange. Like mixing together paint." She stared at the flames intently before her eyes snapped up to meet his. "To what do I owe the pleasure?"

"We found them out in the dandelion fields," one of their captors declared.

For a moment, their leader considered them with a blank expression. She squinted. "What are you three doing so far from home?" Her voice was firm, yet kind, a combination Tor had only ever seen in his mother.

"We're on a quest," Melda said. "To get rid of a curse." She held out her arm in lieu of any explanation.

The woman winced. "A shame," she said. Then, she locked her hands together, "I am Claudia, leader of the giantesses. We serve all living things on the island, promoting peace." She motioned for the other women to cut away the trio's ties, and they did, each of them using a curved knife as long as Tor's forearm. The rope fell away with a slicing sound that made him wince. He rubbed his wrists, relieved to be released, his skin a bit raw.

Claudia lowered her chin. "Now, tell us how we can be of service to you."

Tor looked over at Melda and Engle, then pulled *The Book of Cuentos* out of his backpack. It was worth a shot. The giantesses likely knew the land surrounding their compound better than anyone. Something in the next monster story might sound familiar.

He flipped to the following chapter and read its title. Yes, this next tale could be summarized fairly easily, he thought. "Do you know of a woman spirit that wanders around crying?"

The giantesses looked at each other, confusion drawn across their faces. Claudia raised a perfectly arched eyebrow. "A woman who cries?"

Melda stepped forward, clearly thinking Tor was

doing a bad job at describing the tale. "Maybe you've heard unexplained sobs somewhere? Perhaps in a well or in an old structure?" They remained silent. "In the legend, the woman wanders around Emblem Island, mourning her lost children."

Engle snorted. "Yeah, children she almost *killed*."

The giantesses gasped, horrified. Claudia's eyes narrowed. "And just what is this horrible story called?" she asked, voice stern. "I've never heard of such a dark tale."

"'The Weeping Woman,'" Tor responded quietly. Perhaps it was a mistake asking about it. It was clear they had offended their captors-turned-hosts.

One of the giantesses' faces lit up. She was younger than the rest, with braids styled into a pile on top of her head. A moment later, her expression faltered. "Oh—never mind."

"What is it, Lara?" Claudia prodded.

The girl cleared her throat. "Did you say weeping *woman*?" she asked. Tor nodded. Her face flushed pink. "Oh, I thought you said weeping *willow*, my mistake."

Melda chewed at the inside of her mouth. "Wait, there's a weeping willow tree around here?"

She nodded. "Hundreds of them. An entire forest—Willow Wood."

Melda's eyes brightened. She grabbed the storybook from

Tor's hands, then flipped a few pages, tapping her foot as she tore through "The Weeping Woman" story.

"Come on..." she mumbled. "It's here somewhere..."

Finally, she seemed to have found what she was looking for, because she exclaimed, "Aha!" and jabbed her finger against the thick parchment. "There."

The sentence beneath Melda's finger read:

The woman's cries seeped into the trees and birds around her, who echoed her weeping.

"The weeping woman's cries *seeped* into the trees," she explained. "*Weeping* willows, get it? A forest of them must be exactly where we'd find her." Melda rummaged through Tor's backpack for the map, then opened it up. "Now we just have to locate it..."

They watched as Melda consulted the map's key, looking for the forest symbol. It turned out to be—no surprise—a tree.

It didn't take long for her to spot the marking painted right beside Garth, the giantess settlement. "Willow Wood isn't on the map by name, but if you say the forest is around here, then it must be this one."

One of the giantesses looked over Melda's shoulder, at the tree symbol. "That looks about right."

Melda snapped the map closed. "So, it's settled. We

have to go through those woods to get to..." She took a deep, nervous breath. "To get to where we're going." Tor noticed she avoided saying *Night Witch* for once and wondered why.

The young giantess grinned widely, clearly excited at having been of assistance.

Claudia nodded, then slapped her hands together sharply. "Now that we've been able to lend aid—and have established you're not a threat," a corner of her lips lifted. "How about some lunch?"

Engle practically squealed in delight.

The giantesses watched Engle eat with mild amusement. They had been led into the town's dining hall just a few minutes before and had already been presented with various plates of colossus vegetables. According to Claudia, there was a special garden behind Garth that grew food big enough for a giantess. Engle was in the process of skinning an arm-sized corn on the cob raw.

One of the women raised an eyebrow. "Do you not feed him?"

Melda almost choked on a marble-sized bitterberry. "We feed him a little *too* much."

The beautiful woman tilted her head to the side. "He eats more than we do."

"Tell me about it."

Melda had finished her meal and was sneaking glances at the knife sticking out of a pouch on the woman's waist. It hung over her skirt and sandals, both fashioned from thick leather.

The giantess had caught her staring. "Do you want to hold it?"

Melda flushed pink. "Oh, no. I was just looking."

The giantess stood. "Come," she said, her voice deep and raspy. "Let us show you."

"Show me what?"

"How to wield a weapon."

Melda's mouth fell open, shocked. She recovered quickly and nodded, before following three of the women out of the dining hut. Tor trailed after, curious to see what would happen. Right outside they passed a man, the first they had seen at Garth, who looked incredibly small in contrast to the giantesses. He gave them a polite nod.

"Here." They had reached a sprawling field of white grass, and the giantess held out a sword for Melda to take.

She reached for it tentatively, and almost toppled forward when it was in her grip. The weapon was clearly much heavier than it looked, made of solid metal.

"Like this," the woman said, planting her feet firmly, digging her heel so far that the ground spat up pale dirt. Her knees bent slightly. Then, she gripped the weapon, one hand above the other.

Melda nodded and copied the giantess's stance. Or, at least tried to.

The woman looked impressed. "That's excellent," she said.

Melda held her head up high.

"Now, fight me."

Melda's confident expression disappeared in an instant. She hesitated then said, "Um, no, I don't think I'm ready for that." She threw a worried glance in Tor's direction. The woman didn't seem to have heard her. She yelled out a warrior's cry, then swung forward, knocking her sword against Melda's.

The metal collided, creating a slicing sound that made an earthquake of chills erupt up and down Tor's back.

Nonetheless, when the giantess struck again, Melda moved her sword to the side—and blocked it.

"Confidence is everything," the woman said, as their weapons clashed a third time. She jumped to the side, as light on her toes as a cat. "Believe you'll win, and you just might."

Melda smiled. She charged forward, then sent her weapon down, toward the giantess's toned stomach. The woman laughed in approval, dodging the blow, then sending another one Melda's way.

The other giantesses cheered them on, clapping by clicking their silver swords together.

"I like your necklace," the giantess said, deflecting a hit from Melda. "But it's a liability in battle. Someone could choke you with it."

Melda turned her blade to the side, groaning as she blocked an advance. "Oh. I never take it off."

The giantess smiled. "That's fine. Just tuck it away." She expertly twirled the weapon in her hands before sending it forward again. "You see, a warrior always assesses their opponent's weaknesses. Weakness for one is opportunity for another."

Tor thought about that. Could the Night Witch possibly have a weakness?

Before long, the heavy blade drooped in Melda's grip— she *was* sparring a giantess. The warrior set the tip of her own sword into the ground and bowed. "Good fight," she said. "I'm Valentina."

"I'm Grimelda," Melda said, returning the bow. When she looked up, her teeth were bared in a fierce grin, one Tor had never seen before. Then she said, "Teach me more."

As Melda learned the finer points of sword fighting, Tor decided to wander. He passed another man in the market who seemed to be pounding metal into different shapes—possibly for body armor. All at once, the blacksmith dropped the hammer he had been using and started to twist the gleaming material with his bare hands. The emblem on his arm jumped out as his bicep flexed and bulged: the mark for strength.

There were several different categories of gifts a person could be born with. Strength fell into the classification of warrior emblems. Anyone born with a mark that could make them useful in battle had a responsibility to fight, should a war take place—at least, that's what his mother had told him. Instead of schooling, these children were sometimes sent to Garth, to be trained in battle by the giantesses.

When Tor was a small child, long before he had discovered swimming, he used to wish *he* had been blessed with a warrior emblem...

He locked his jaw. He had always wanted more—and look where that had gotten him.

"You seem troubled."

Tor whirled around to see Claudia, the giantess leader, standing a few feet away.

He tried to deny it, but she saw right through him. "Take a walk with me," she said.

The people of Garth nodded as Claudia strode down the street, in a less severe form of a bow. Tor wondered what she had done to earn their respect. For the giantesses, power was not passed down by generation, or even by emblem, but was earned through honorable feats in battle.

"Something worries you," she said.

"Why would you say that?"

"Eyes are a window to the brain, they betray our deepest, darkest thoughts—and *your* brain looks troubled."

Tor wondered if there was a mind-reading emblem hidden somewhere beneath her sleeve. "I've been given a task I'm sure I can't complete," he admitted.

She nodded. Paused for a few moments. "Is it honorable, what you've been asked to do?"

Tor considered that. Killing someone did not seem honorable at all, no matter how he looked at it. Even if he needed to, in self-defense, or in the defense of another, he still would not find that act noble—only necessary.

Still, this was the *Night Witch*. A person responsible for hundreds of people's deaths, maybe more. In killing her, he could be saving lives she would have taken otherwise.

Was *that* honorable?

He turned to look Claudia right in her dark eyes. "I've been tasked with killing someone," he said. "Someone who deserves it, but a person nonetheless."

The woman did not look shocked. Of course she didn't, Tor thought. She was a warrior.

"How do you do it?" he asked. Then, he thought of a better question. "How do you *live* with it?"

Claudia sighed. They were stopped at the edge of town, and she leaned against a hut, looking at the sky. She squinted, and dozens of wrinkles sprouted from the corners of her eyes, making Tor think she might have been much older than he first thought. "The same way one lives with a disease. Every day, it eats you up just a little more." She clicked her tongue. "But, in the end, you must find a way to go on." Claudia faced Tor then, her expression turning solemn. "If you don't, it'll swallow you whole."

● ☽ ◗ ☾

That night, they slept in tiny huts, made specifically for visitors. Though their accommodations were much more comfortable than the stones they had slept on the night before, Tor could not find it in himself to close his eyes. He stared at the ceiling, the wood expertly woven into a pliable material, thinking about Claudia's words.

When he had asked his question, he had hoped she would tell him it was easy—that killing someone who deserved it would not leave even the smallest stain on his conscience.

But, if anything, she had made him feel worse.

He couldn't kill anyone, even the witch, he knew that for certain.

There had to be another way.

In the morning they ate with the rest of the giantesses, who were getting ready to set out on an expedition. Tor had watched them carry their giant bows and arrows on their backs like they weighed nothing. Melda sat next to Valentina, who was in the middle of telling them about the time she had run across a lake of quicksand, barefoot.

"Weren't you afraid you'd sink?" Melda asked.

She shrugged. "Of course. But why would I let that stop me?"

Melda grinned. "I've been meaning to ask. What are those bands on your arms?" She pointed to places that looked like they had been painted on, just like Koso's markings.

Valentina lifted her sleeve. "They're warrior signs. You earn one for every honorable mission you complete." She pointed to one. "I earned this when I was ten. There was a beast terrorizing a village to the west. So I got on my horse and went to find it."

Engle sat back in his chair. "You killed a beast when you were ten?"

Valentina smiled. "No." She pointed toward something Tor hadn't noticed until then—a long scar that ran down her neck from her jaw to her collarbone. "I earned the sign because I was brave enough to try."

On their way out of the dining hut, the giantess cook gave Engle a sack filled with wrapped-up slices of bread, jams, and vegetables. More than enough to last them a few days...if Engle didn't eat it all within the first hour, that was.

On their way out, Tor overheard Valentina tell Melda, "Come visit us whenever you would like." Then, she pulled something from her pocket. It was a silver ring, the same color as the band on the giantess's arm. She handed it to Melda. "And remember. There are many ways to be strong that don't require a sword."

The Weeping Woman

O nce upon a family secret, a man rode through a village on horseback. He had slicked hair and wore boots that were scratched all over, telling the stories of his many adventures.

The man on horseback stopped at a tavern. When he entered, everyone turned to look. Visitors were rare.

One of the villagers saw an opportunity. He walked over to the man and said, "If what you search is a place to finally rest your boots, I know a most incredible woman, who is kind, intelligent, and in search of a new chapter of her life."

"Where might I find such a partner?" the man asked.

"In the house next to my own. She is my daughter."

The man hurried home to warn his family. "He looks to be very wealthy," he said. "And he has a horse."

The daughter had dreams of leaving her small village and living in a big house, with food served to her every hour and people under her command. She was not kind, as her father had boasted, but she *was* cunning. And she had been gifted an emblem that could prove especially useful. One that allowed her to convince anyone to fall in love with her. Though the effects did not last forever, the woman did not care. All she needed was enough time to get everything she had always wished for.

So, the man on horseback and the woman were married. And, a few springs later, she had given birth to two children. Instead of whisking her away to a distant land, they stayed in that same village. And it seemed as though the man's only valuable possession was his horse. Still, the woman found that even without money, she cared for her husband. As the years ticked by, she wondered if his feelings for her could possibly be true.

One wintery day the effects of her emblem wore off, and the man realized he was not, and never had been, in love. He rode away on his horse while the stars still shined, leaving his family behind.

Overcome with sadness, the woman took her children to a nearby river. She decided she would rather perish than carry on—and would take her children with her.

She walked into the water, holding their hands, intending to drown them and herself. But, before they were submerged, her children escaped.

The woman wanted to find them, to bring them back—but she had been in the water too long. She found she could not feel the frost of the river on her cheeks. Her toes could not feel the stones beneath her feet. Instead of swimming, she now floated, right out of the water.

The woman's cries seeped into the trees and birds around her, who echoed her weeping.

She roams the island in search of children to take for her own. She lures them with pity, so that she may not be forever alone.

14

WILLOW WOOD

They stood in front of a long-armed weeping willow, the first of hundreds spread out behind it, all hunched over like a gathering of old women. Its dense, cascading leaves were white, like everything else around them.

"It's beautiful," Melda said, at the same time Engle exclaimed, "It looks like a swamp monster."

Melda rolled her eyes. Then she gasped softly, looking around. "Do you hear that?" she asked.

Tor didn't.

"No, really, it sounds like it's coming from the *willow*." She walked up to the tree and reached out a hand to touch its leaves, which hung like a curtain.

As soon as Melda stepped close enough, the willow's limp branches suddenly came alive.

They wrapped around her body, swallowing her up.

"Melda!" Engle yelled, just as Tor ran forward. He jumped through the thick foliage and promptly collided with something solid. *The trunk?*

"Ow!" No. Melda.

She stood very still, branches encircling her body the same way a boa constrictor might. But instead of suffocating her, the tree's movements seemed more like a caress.

"Come here, and be quiet about it," Melda whispered. He bent all the way toward her, inhaling the faint fruity perfume of the tree. "Listen," she instructed.

With his ear pressed against the leaves, Tor could finally hear it, too: a low crying. Not just *crying*, but the type of sobbing that came straight from the chest and left everyone around the poor soul feeling shattered.

He swallowed, throat dry. "What is that?" It couldn't be the weeping woman. The cries were coming straight out of the tree itself. Unless she was trapped inside it...

The woman's cries seeped into the trees and birds around her, who echoed her weeping.

Tor yanked the branches holding Melda, and they recoiled, setting her free. "Let's keep moving," he said. "She might be close by."

They walked through the forest of mammoth weeping

willows, some extending their branches as they passed, like mothers wanting an embrace, and others shivering from their tops all the way to the ground, the sound reminding Tor of wind chimes.

Engle kept watch. "I don't see much, on account of all of these leaves. But I still haven't spotted the crying woman yet," he said.

"*Weeping* woman," Melda corrected. "*Weeping.*"

"Same thing."

"It absolutely is not."

Suddenly, Engle stopped.

"What is it?" Tor asked.

"I'm not sure what...but something's moving."

"What?"

"Something's moving just at the corner of my vision—"

All at once, every single weeping willow shed its leaves. Tor blinked, and the view in the woods was suddenly unobstructed, the previously bare ground now covered in a blanket of white.

Engle gulped. "Well, that...clears things up."

Melda rushed toward one of the willows, placing a gentle hand on its trunk. "Do you think it wept all of its leaves away?" she asked, voice full of concern.

Engle shrugged. "Maybe."

They plowed ahead, weaving around the bare trees, and soon came upon a lake that sat still as stone, a few white leaves sprinkled on its surface. And there was something else.

"Do you see that?" Engle asked, his voice cracking like firewood.

A woman hovered just a foot above the pond. She wore a long, white dress that floated behind her like silk underwater, with delicate buttons that reached her neck. Her hair was dark as a raven's feather, and she combed it with a clam just as a deep sob spilled out of her mouth.

As if sensing their presence, the woman turned to look right at Engle, Tor, and Melda, who had not moved an inch.

Her mouth parted, letting out another cry.

It pained him. Tor swallowed. He suddenly had a deep urge to walk toward the grieving woman. To comfort her. To step a foot into the water, and swim toward her...

"Ow!" he yelped, as Engle grabbed his arm. He turned to shake him off.

"She'll drown you if you get any closer," Engle whispered.

Tor looked back at the lake and jumped in horror. The woman was right in front of him, her long-nailed fingers reaching toward his cheek. Her face was twisted in pain, water dripping from her hair in a puddle beneath her floating feet.

He kept staring at her, cries ringing through his ears, as

Engle pulled him away. She did not follow, tears flowing down her cheeks as she watched them leave. They kept going until the ground turned from white to gray, and Willow Wood was long behind them.

They walked through the sparse woods in silence, and Tor tried to appreciate what color there was, knowing from the map they had just a few miles to go before reaching the darkness that was the Shadows. A heavy mist descended, enveloping them in its damp grayness—a sure sign they were getting close.

So why did it feel like they were still so far away?

Tor tensed, a knot of dread tightening in his stomach. The woods around them might have been quiet, but Tor couldn't escape the wail of the weeping woman, her cries echoing in his head, filling him with an aching sadness and guilt for walking away.

He needed a lake, a river, a pond even—anything he could plunge into to wipe his mind clean. Without water to help wash his troubles away, worries and fears stacked up like swaying piles of glass plates.

And they were about to come crashing down.

They had reached a roughly plowed field of dirt that extended all the way to the outskirts of a thick forest. Tor did not think it was possible, but it had become quieter than before. Even from a few feet away, they heard nothing. No animal sounds, no indication as to what they would find inside the woods. Just as the know-all had said, it seemed as though most creatures had fled the frigid darkness. Goose bumps ran up and down his arms as he looked over Melda's shoulder, at the map she held with trembling hands.

They had officially reached the Shadows.

The forest was painted in dark shades, from the dark brown bushes to the deep green grass. Everything looked as though it had been touched by night, though it was barely afternoon.

"Well, this is depressing," Engle said.

He was right. As they walked on, Tor thought to himself that the Shadows had an energy to it, a negative aura that weighed everything down. The farther they walked, the worse his mood became.

It all seemed helpless.

"I'm not hungry," Engle said, breaking the cold silence. He said it though no one had asked if he was. His voice was flat. "I'm just—not."

Neither was Tor. He wasn't *anything*. No, that was wrong. He was irritated. Angry.

He ground his molars, a tornado of dark thoughts wreaking havoc in his mind. Doubts taunted him like ghosts, appearing and disappearing, driving him mad.

After a couple of miles, the woods stopped altogether, as if it could not be bothered to fill up that particular stretch of land. The ground was cracked all over, in scales. Like they were walking over a giant creature's back.

Soon, just as it had stopped, the forest returned.

Daylight faded away, yet it seemed as though they had been walking for no time at all. Or maybe it felt like forever. Tor couldn't decide.

His foot caught on a root, and he flew forward, landing hard on his stomach and knocking the wind from his chest. He lay in the dirt gasping, taking in a massive network of roots, now at eye level. The forest was full of them.

"Are you okay?" Melda asked, offering him a hand. He didn't take it. Instead, he stayed splayed out on the cold ground.

Tor had never felt farther from home than he did now. How long had they been gone? Had he lost track?

Days. Tor thought about his parents for the first time in a long time, about what they must be going through. Their son was missing, after all. *Off on an adventure.*

Would they have gone looking for him? Had the Chieftess

ordered the village to drop all of their responsibilities in favor of searching for Estrelle's lost children?

"Tor?" Melda's hand still hovered in front of his face.

"No," Tor said, getting up himself.

At the hermit's hut, an adventure had sounded honorable. Necessary. Now, it sounded foolish.

"No to what?" Melda asked, her eyes annoyingly filled with concern.

"To everything," Tor yelled, surprising himself with the sharp tone of his voice. "What were we thinking? How could we believe that we could stop a witch? That I could *kill* her?"

He shook his head. He couldn't do it. Tor had planned on finding a way to convince the witch to reverse the curse—but so far, he hadn't thought of anything. Even if they survived the rest of the journey, they were walking toward a doomed mission.

"I'm done. I'm going back."

Melda blinked. "What?"

"You heard me."

"But what about the curse?" She took a step forward. "What about your Grail?" Her sleeve almost ripped as she yanked it up to display the mark on her wrist. "This isn't just about you. What about us?"

Tor set his jaw. "Someone in the village will know what

to do. Someone older, someone more experienced. If we take a hopper, or a horse, we could make it back before it's too late. We know the way now." What had he been thinking, going off like this? Had he actually believed he could find the Night Witch, the horrible figure from all of those stories? The one that he hadn't even known existed, up until a few days ago? He was nobody. A born leader who had wished his emblem away. He might as well spend his last days with the people he loved, with Rosa.

Engle and Melda stood fixed in place.

Tor's nostrils flared. "Well? Are you coming or not?" He took one step back toward the weeping willows and Garth and Frostflake and everywhere they'd been. Back toward home.

Engle looked at Melda for just a moment. Then, he sighed and stepped forward, to the space beside Tor.

"And you?" Tor said.

Melda straightened her shoulders. "I'm going to find the witch."

Engle blinked. "Alone?"

"If that's what it takes."

Tor sighed. "You can't be serious. You'll get yourself killed."

"Then give me the dagger." Melda's hands were shaking, but something in her expression was resolute, hard as marble.

Tor knew with one look he would never be able to convince her otherwise.

Without saying a word, Tor handed it over. She gripped its hilt, nodded once, then disappeared into the shadows.

"Wait!" Tor said, but there was no response. They took a few steps deeper into the woods, but the trees were too thick, and the fog was too good at lending cover. Dread and regret filled Tor's chest in equal measure.

What on Emblem had he done?

"She's gone," Engle said.

THE SILVER FALCON'S FEATHER

O nce upon a haunted wood, a bird wished to see the stars. It flew farther than any other being had, past mountain peaks, clouds, and even the sun. It reached the top of the world, where the sky was black. The stars blinked hello.

Your silver color is the greatest shade I have ever seen, the bird said to the stars.

Take a bath in the moon, and you, too, can shine just as brightly, they replied.

The bird dipped its wings inside the puddle of moon, and they came out glimmering as radiantly as freshly polished swords.

When the bird returned home, it found its new beauty had been a curse. It was hunted by islanders, hoping to take the bird down, wishing to keep the shining feathers for themselves. So, the bird remained hidden in the shadows. Until, one day, it heard the scream of a little girl who had fallen into a river in an attempt to save her sister.

The bird swooped down and carried both girls to safety. Then, it gifted the sister one of its feathers.

One feather, one wish, it said, wanting to reward the girl's bravery.

Over time, the silver falcon gave a handful of its feathers away. And, many years later, inspired the wish-gods to do the same.

And so Eve was created.

15

A DARK FOREST

Tor and Engle were very quiet as they made their way toward Garth. Engle had his head down and was kicking up more dirt with his shoes than usual.

Though his friend said nothing, Tor could practically read his thoughts.

"She *chose* to keep going," he said. "She made a choice."

Engle nodded.

"She's stubborn. No changing her mind, even though she's going to get herself killed out there." Tor's stomach sank as he realized just how true his words were. They had taken all of the resources; his backpack suddenly weighed a thousand pounds, every last bit of food and every last sip of water a reminder that Melda didn't stand a chance. "She should have come with us," he said softly.

Still, Engle didn't speak, he just kept kicking at the ground, like uprooting black flowers would solve their problems.

"I feel bad, but we *did* ask her to. It's not like we could have made her change her mind."

Engle gave a simple *mm-hmm* that did nothing to settle Tor's guilt-ridden brain. He knew very well it was his fault Melda even had reason to find the witch in the first place.

Still, it was not *all* his fault, another part of his mind reminded him. *She* was the one who touched the eye on his wrist, after all.

"You know what? She'll probably be fine. I mean, it's Melda. She's about the most capable person we know."

Engle sighed. "If you say so."

They walked on and as the negative weight of the Shadows started to lift, Tor became very aware of an especially painful thought. Even though his mother was an esteemed Chieftess, and he himself had been born with her emblem, Tor was the worst leader in the world.

He had led his friends into a doomed mission.

And then he had given up.

Tor and Engle were almost to Garth when they heard an earsplitting scream.

They groaned; Tor gritted his teeth. The sound ripped through his brain like a lightning bolt had traveled through one ear and out the next. The source was immediately familiar.

"Melda," they cried at once.

Tor and Engle turned around immediately, running back through the forest. They ran quickly, expecting to come across their friend at any moment. They yelled her name, over and over.

But, after a few minutes, they stopped.

"Wait," Tor said. "We've been walking for hours. If Melda kept going, there's no way we would have heard her scream."

Engle's face was flushed. "But we did," he said between gulps of air, reaching up to brush his light brown hair out of his face. "It sounded like she was right in front of—"

Tor grabbed Engle's arm before he could finish, ignoring Engle's yelp. He held his wrist up right next to it; the eye there was fluttering, as if in warning. "What if the curse connects us? What if Melda's voice was projected through that?" He nodded toward the lips on Engle's arm.

Engle gulped. "Then I would say that Melda has found herself in big trouble."

Engle and Tor were doubled over, panting. They had run for an hour straight. Tor dug underneath his rib, hoping it would stop the cramping, but it did nothing but pinch his skin.

"We're never going to find her," he said. "Not in these woods."

Engle squinted, searching the distance. Then, he sighed. There was nothing but trees and fog for miles.

Tor planted his hand against a trunk, sweat dripping down his forehead even though the air had turned ice-cold.

Melda was gone. She had been captured...or eaten by a creature they hadn't yet encountered. He thought of the remaining *Cuentos* stories and paled. "The Faceless Man" was one of them—about a spirit known for stealing faces to wear as masks.

Bile rose in his throat. They had no hope of finding her.

And it was all his fault.

All of it.

How could he be so senseless? So weak? So selfish? He never should have let her go alone. Not after she had saved him countless times.

Not after she had become his friend.

Engle stiffened beside him.

"What is it?" Tor straightened.

His friend smiled so wide his freckles stretched thin. "I think I see something."

Engle raced ahead, his breath coming out in frantic white puffs as the air became somehow even colder. Tor followed, willing his legs to move when all they wanted to do was collapse underneath him.

He found Engle standing over an object coated in dirt. Still, even in the darkness, the blue stuck out like a sore thumb.

Melda's drop of color.

Engle took it gently into his palm. "Someone has her," he said, pointing at a trail of wagon wheel marks Tor could barely make out and would have definitely missed on his own.

She still might be alive.

"We're going to find her," Tor said resolutely. All they had to do was follow the tracks.

There was a worried fold between Engle's eyebrows as he nodded. "Yes. But first, we're going to need a plan."

● ◡ ◗ ◖

The tower where Melda had been taken looked ready to topple over. Paint had been scraped away, and bricks had fallen altogether. Windows were blocked by iron. Men stood outside of it, holding weapons, talking loudly. There was a faint smell of meat cooking nearby.

Their plan had been simple. Or, at least, it *appeared*

simple before one of the fireworks they set off shot itself into the forest. Now, a small fire was growing into a big one, the smoke reminding Tor of Eve.

"Come on," Engle whispered. He had seen the barrels of fireworks from a mile away, and came to the conclusion they would make the best distraction—and cover. And he was right. Their steps went unheard as they ran from behind the dense thicket of trees to the base of the tower. "The man with the keys has a big potbelly and is missing the top of his hair." According to Engle, Melda had been locked in a cell.

"There," he said, and Tor swallowed. Because the man Engle had pointed out was walking right toward them.

"And who are you two?" he demanded.

Tor wanted to punch him right in the mouth for daring to kidnap his friend, but the man would be hard to take down. And he and Engle weren't exactly known for their fighting skills.

So, just like Mrs. Alma had repeated over and over again in leadership class, Tor knew he had to change his tactics. He forced his scowl into a smile. "We're here looking for work."

The man's wrinkle-inscribed forehead crinkled even more. He barked out a laugh, reminding Tor that his gift of persuasion had been taken away along with his emblem. "*Work?* Doing what? Moving a stack of hay around the property?" The man grabbed his stomach with both hands and laughed again.

Tor and Engle shared a concerned look. It didn't seem as though his tactic was working very well.

The large man's eyes narrowed. "Say, what's on your wrist?" he said. He took a step toward Tor, and Tor took a step back. They repeated this twice before the man seemed to get impatient and charged at Tor, managing to grab his arm so tightly Tor was actually afraid the bone might snap in half.

"Let me see what's on your wrist, boy!" he yelled.

Tor struggled, or at least tried to, until the man elbowed him right in the ribs.

He bent over, gasping, the air sucked right out of him.

When the red-faced man finally did see what Tor had been hiding—the cursed eye blinking hello—he opened his mouth wide in fear. But before he could speak a word, the kidnapper made a grunting noise, blinked, and fell to the ground.

Engle stood there, *The Book of Cuentos* still held high above his head.

Tor did not waste a moment, grabbing the ring of keys right from the passed-out man's belt.

Engle looked at the heavy book in his hands, then shrugged, a small grin on his face. "This book really *is* useful."

The two boys raced through the tower, stopping at each door to peer inside. Finally they found the right one, which held a collection of cells. When they reached Melda's, she jumped up from a filthy, hay-covered floor and gripped the solid metal bars keeping her caged, her face pale. For once, it seemed like she was at a loss for words.

Then, she found some. "You should go," she said, craning her head to peer down the hallway. "The guard will come back any minute."

Engle laughed as Tor produced the ring of keys. "That guard isn't going anywhere anytime soon." Melda opened her mouth but didn't say a thing as he opened the door and grabbed her hand, pulling her down the twisting stairs and into the hall below.

"Who are these people?" Engle asked quietly. There were yells for water outside. It seemed like their distraction was still working.

"Emblem-thieves," Melda said, hands in fists by her sides.

Tor's jaw locked. Emblem-thieves were markless people who killed to inherit another's power. His mother had warned him as a child never to veer from the main road, lest he come across them.

"How did you find me?" she whispered.

Engle grinned. He held up something in his hand—her

necklace. "And our linked curse may have had something to do with it."

Though the woods were on fire, and they were still surrounded by armed men, Melda did something surprising—she smiled. "I thought I'd never see it again." She put the glowing pendant back on with care, then threw her arms around Tor and Engle. "Thank you—you have no idea... I..."

When she pulled away, both boys were flushed red.

The hall below the tower had walls made of stones that appeared to be held together by caked-up dirt. The tables were covered by a thin layer of dust, and the chairs wore spiderwebs between their legs. It seemed to be empty, everyone outside battling the quickly spreading fire.

Tor heard a whisper.

"Hello?" it said.

He looked at Melda and she froze, like she had heard it, too. The sound came from the back of the room, which led to a dimly lit corridor. Tor didn't think; he walked directly toward it, Melda matching him step for step.

"What are you doing?" Engle grabbed at his arm. "Let's get out of here."

Tor wasn't going anywhere—not until he knew whose voice had spoken. It had sounded so sad, so broken. "Just a minute," he said, shaking him off.

Melda did what any good leader would do. She delegated. "Why don't you go find us some more food?" she asked. Engle hesitated for a moment, then went off to search the kitchens.

Tor and Melda inched forward, careful not to make a noise, should it be a trap.

They entered the corridor, which consisted of bare walls and a few torches to light their way. Then, the hallway opened up, and there were cells, just like the one Melda had been trapped in. And they were not empty.

Dozens of people, young and old, sat on piles of hay—sad faces behind locked gates. Some barely glanced at Melda and Tor; others' expressions lit up. A boy their age rushed to the bars, holding the metal tightly.

"Help us," he said. "Help us get out of here."

Tor fumbled with the ring of keys he had stolen.

Melda bent down so she met the boy's eyes. "What happened to you?"

"They came to our village," he said. "North of The Plains. Took anyone with a valuable emblem." Tor watched as she looked down, undoubtedly searching for his marking.

"You're a *painter*," she said. Tor had never met one before. They could paint anything to look as true as real life.

The painter smiled sadly.

"Why haven't you tried to escape? Surely you could have painted a key?"

He sighed. "We've tried. Something in these cells blocks our power." *How was that even possible?*

Tor finally found the right key out of dozens, and the door swung open.

"Come on," Melda said, urging him out. "I can't believe they did this to you," she whispered. Tor saw that the boy's wrists were hurt—rings of skin seemed to have been peeled off, no doubt by tight restraints that had stayed on too long.

"Why are you surprised? The people here are dark-hearted."

Tor gritted her teeth. "Why?" There had to be a reason. People were not simply born this evil.

"It's the Night Witch," the painter said quietly, as if the wicked woman could hear them. "When an evil so pure exists, it seeps into its surroundings. Tarnishes everything around it."

The Night Witch. Of course she was responsible for this.

Tor's hands shook as he hurried to find the right keys to each cell. Each door required a different one, making the task much harder than expected. Still, his fingers moved at lightning speed. Every moment he wasted could be one that they would be discovered, he told himself, chanting it in his head like a spell.

As he reached the last door, he locked eyes with a woman holding a baby on her knee. She was covered in dirt, all the way from her ankles to her eyelashes. Even the baby looked like it hadn't bathed in days.

Why would those men take a child so young?

Then he saw the little boy's emblem: a snowflake.

Clattering sounds at the other end of the corridor caught his attention. The prisoners he had already freed started to retreat back into the hallway.

They'd been found out.

Tor hurried to unlock the final door, then worked his way through the crowd to Melda. She protected the entire group with her arms, splayed out in a T.

"You're not getting anywhere near them," she said, her voice so resolute Tor almost believed her. But he saw how many men had gathered at the mouth of the hall. Dozens of them, all holding something sharp enough to tear through flesh.

No. He had to come up with a new plan, had to do something. Another distraction! Or maybe Engle had finished in the kitchen and was cooking up a scheme that very moment. He had gotten them in—maybe he could get them out, too.

Melda spoke again. "You've mistreated these people long enough," she said, her steady voice echoing off the stone walls. "Their emblems are not yours to take." She turned her head for just a moment. "You are released!" she yelled at the crowd behind her. "Let us show these thieves exactly what we can do."

Just like that, the words coated in her magic, the crowd behind her shed their fears like snakes discarding old, broken skin. A woman cried out and leapt forward, taking down a guard in a single motion. A flurry of others followed. Tor stood transfixed as a teenage girl disappeared right before his eyes, then reappeared after having struck a thief in the head with a bucket. An old man with a telekinesis emblem threw a chair at another.

One of their captors threw a pike, but it was blocked by a woman who snapped it in half with her bare hands. The painter used dirt from the ground to draw a sword on his arm, which peeled off into a real metal one. He used it to fight off a thief holding an axe.

But there were still too many. The prisoners, Melda at their front, were pushed farther and farther down the hall, sharp pikes just inches from their stomachs. Tor closed his eyes in spite of himself, one of the weapons just a foot from his skull.

It was over.

The dust-covered woman from the last cell emerged from the back of the crowd, carrying her crying baby. One guard moved toward them, but before he could do anything, the child with the snowflake emblem lifted his hand and everything went very quiet.

At once, all of the remaining thieves were frozen solid.

Silence.

The group of former prisoners erupted in cheers, throwing their arms around each other. Engle surprised Tor by poking his head up from behind a turned-over table, breadbasket in hand.

Before escaping into the night, dozens of the formerly imprisoned people stopped to thank Melda. One woman even bowed low and whispered, "Thank you for helping us find our courage."

A young man with a shaved head approached them. "Come with us," he offered. "We're from a village in the west called Fluska."

Melda smiled. "Thank you," she said. She looked over at Tor and Engle earnestly. "But we have our own journey still ahead of us."

"Then, please, allow me to give you a token of our appreciation." He produced a coin from his pocket, one that looked nothing like a dobble. It was silver and had a spiral in the middle, with a more intricate design on the edges. Tor knew it right away. The emblem for teleportation.

"You're a *telecorp!*" Engle yelled.

The man nodded with a flicker of amusement in his eyes. He pressed the coin against the top of his arm, where a similar spiral sat—enchanting it, so that the object captured a bit of his emblem's power. The young man winced, for it was not a pleasant process, and the token glowed for just a moment. Then, he placed it in Melda's hand.

"When that journey is over," he said. "This will take you back home."

"Thank you." Melda stared down at the gift in her palm, and Tor imagined his longing for home matched the look of yearning written across her face. But then her eyes hardened, and she slipped the coin into her pocket.

The man nodded and turned to go—then seemed to change his mind. He faced them again. "Forgive me, but not many people go this far into the Shadows by choice. Are you traveling deeper still?"

Melda nodded once.

The telecorp's expression turned solemn. "As you can imagine, my talent allows me to get in and out of places unnoticed. I've spent many a nighttime hour in The Plains' library, reading everything they have on the Shadows.

"So, allow me to give you a warning. Prepare yourselves. It is cold as ice farther inside, the weather as temperamental as a child. A few miles north of where we stand, there is an abandoned mill at the edge of an abandoned village. We passed it on our way. Go there, and prepare," he urged them, eyes gleaming. "Ready yourselves, because the Shadows will test you, body and mind. Forgive me, but people far more capable than you have been tested—and have failed."

The Sun and Moon

Once upon a starlit night, there was a girl with silver hair and eyes like pearls. She came out only after dusk, for she liked the quiet of the darkness.

There was also a boy with golden hair who loved the feeling of heat upon his skin. He adored the outdoors so much, he had trouble sleeping at night, yearning for daytime. It was during one of these restless nights that the boy saw the girl through the glass of his window.

He slipped on his shoes and went outside.

"Where are you going?" he asked, trying to catch up.

She was fast, weaving quietly through the village until she reached the sea. He found her there, on the water's edge, staring so deeply into the ocean that the tip of her silver hair swirled in the sea foam.

"Who are you?" he asked.

Her eyes wide, she jumped up and backed away. "I am no one," she said. "A nightmare, if you let me be."

The boy could not get the girl out of his head. So

the next night, instead of sleeping, he walked to that same sea and found her there.

"You shouldn't have come," she said. And even though she had warned him twice to stay away, the boy sat down beside her.

The boy and girl fell in love. They planned a future together. They left the village and traveled across the island, on adventures like sewn-together dreams, too much like fairy tales to be real.

But the universe did not approve this pairing. They were cursed, never to be together. And the only way to keep them apart was to separate them. Forever.

The girl became the moon, pearl in the sky.

And the boy became the sun, fiery ball of light.

Each dusk and dawn they pass, never to meet again.

Yet, their love never died.

16

THE MILL

By the time they left the tower, it was almost morning. Their backpack full of bread, Engle, Tor, and Melda watched the Fluskas enter the dark forest. The baby with the snowflake emblem stopped what was left of the fire with a single gesture, and the telecorp gave them a sideways wave, as if to say good luck, before disappearing into the foliage.

Tor found he didn't know what to say. What *could* he say? He had abandoned a mission he himself had created and had left one of his friends behind... Guilt ate at him.

They stood for a moment, facing each other in silence.

"I'm sorry," Tor blurted out, at the same time that Melda said, "I hope you're sorry."

Her eyes widened a bit in surprise, like she hadn't expected for him to apologize so easily. "What for?"

"We should have never let you go alone," he admitted. Melda raised her eyebrows, and he added, "We should have never *left* in the first place."

"That's right," she said sharply. The serious set of her mouth softened. Tor noticed how effortlessly Melda could move from firm to empathetic. It was those kinds of things that made people *want* to follow her. And that was the magic of a leadership emblem, after all. Being able to inspire others to join a person in their cause not through force, but through trust and faith.

"The Shadows makes the worst part of ourselves come out, if we let it," she was saying. "But the only way we make it to the Night Witch is together." She sighed. "This isn't about just us anymore."

She was right. As much as Tor wished he could turn back home again, they had a bigger purpose now. If the witch was responsible for the Shadows and its wicked people, she had to be stopped.

"Like the telecorp said, we need to be ready," Melda said. "We haven't slept for almost twenty-four hours, we've hardly had anything to eat, we'll freeze in these clothes if it gets any colder, and, I don't know about you, but I'm sore as a bruised banana." She patted her ribs and winced. "If we have any chance at even *reaching* the witch, we have to be smart. I think

241

we should go to the mill in the abandoned village the telecorp told us about and see if we can find more supplies."

Tor agreed. A few pieces of bread and what was left of the giantess's provisions weren't going to be enough to last them the rest of their journey to the Night Witch.

Worry tightened his chest. Tor knew very well that they weren't just going to the mill for food and rest—the truth was they also didn't know where to go next. The next story mentioned a lake, but even that clue wasn't any help, since the area of the map that marked the Shadows was blank. And it wasn't like they could ask locals for aid.

This far deep into the darkness, the only people they could trust were each other.

●)) (

The abandoned village looked as though a raging fire had burnt a normal town to a crisp. It sat just outside of the woods, each building covered in soot-colored plaster. Flaky gray dirt lined the streets like volcanic sand.

"How could anyone have lived like this?" Engle asked.

Tor wondered the same thing. He thought of the canopy of purple leaves over his house, and all of the blue, yellow, and orange trees under which everyone else lived. The rainbow of birds that filled those trees and sang along with Rosa every morning. *That* was life, he told himself.

This looked like death.

"I don't know. Maybe that's why they left."

They wandered into the modest town square, framed by tiny shops, each with a chimney and two windows. Melda coughed when they opened the first store's door, dust creating a thick cloud. She waved her hands in front of her, ordering it all away. If only she could.

"Well, this solves one of our problems," Melda said. The room they had walked into was filled with stacks of wool, piled high like blankets. A spinning wheel and loom were situated in the back, along with barrels of what looked to be black dye. There were also tables of clothes that had already been finished and neatly folded. Tor looked down at his dirt-covered outfit. There was a hole near his elbow, and on his knee. It *would* be nice to change.

"The telecorp said it would get colder, so we'll need warmer clothing to make it deeper into the Shadows." She picked up a gray shirt and a pair of pants that looked slightly too large. "This should do for a base..." she mumbled to herself. "I'll just have to use some of this extra fabric to make something like a sweater...some warmer socks, if I have time..."

Engle and Tor looked at her, mouths slightly ajar.

"You can make a sweater out of *this*?" Engle asked, motioning toward the fabric and wool.

She nodded sheepishly. "I make all my brothers' clothes," she said in a tiny voice, looking down at the floor. "And my own."

Her expensive-looking clothing suddenly made sense. Still, Tor wondered how Melda possibly had time to make five sets of clothing every time her brothers grew a little more, while also helping to take care of them *and* completing the stacks of assignments Mrs. Alma gave every night. She had never even been late to class once. "Do you sleep, Melda?" he asked.

She shrugged. "Not as much as I should, I suppose."

He scratched the back of his head. "And what should we do?" he said, feeling useless. It was a strange thing, speaking those words. Though he supposed she *was* the only one with a leadership emblem now.

Melda didn't even bat an eye. "I imagine we'll be battling some tough trials as we near the Night Witch. We'll need our strength. Engle, if you could, try to find some stored water. And locate some beds or cots we can sleep on tonight." She turned to Tor. "It would be great if you could visit each building and then the mill. See if there are any weapons, food that hasn't spoiled yet, or other resources we can use."

Then, with a deep breath, she started combing through the piles of gray clothing.

Engle and Tor parted ways in what used to be the town square. Abandoned carts had been turned over, ash-coated rats scurrying around their wheels. Tor was almost reassured by the sight of the vermin; at least *something* was alive here.

He entered a small shop with a bell at the top of the door. It jangled loudly, making him jump.

Rolls of parchment sat behind the counter, some of it dyed different shades like lavender, honey, rose, and teal. It was a paper store. He studied them, surprised. This far into the Shadows, he hadn't expected to see so much color.

With no time to waste, Tor grabbed a piece of wound-up parchment, an ink pot, and a quill, deciding to use it to keep track of anything useful he might find.

The next store seemed to have been a tavern in its prime. The entire interior was crafted in reddish mahogany, from the long bar to the chairs that had been stacked into neat piles. Each step Tor took was matched by a gust of dust, making him sneeze. The place reminded him of the pub in Cristal Town. *Emblem, was that only a few days ago?* Tor thought. It seemed like forever.

In a back storage room, he spotted a tank of water. He made note of it on his paper, then moved on to the next shop.

Tor visited a total of ten different stores, each surprisingly intact and filled with different artisanal products. He found leather boots in one place, a dozen gloves in another, a gold pocket watch, and even a wheel of cheese that had, unfortunately, gone bad long ago. Funny, Tor had thought that cheese was one of those things that got better with age, but this particular one had crumbled into a sour-smelling powder the consistency of sand. He took another whiff just to be sure and almost lost the small amount that *was* in his stomach. No, he thought, leaving the store at once. Definitely not edible.

With each new discovery, Tor began to question more and more why the people of the town had left behind such valuable objects.

It almost seemed as if the village had been abandoned overnight. But why?

At last, he stood in front of the mill. It was the biggest one he had ever seen, the door taller than three of him combined. Inside was even more of a surprise. Though it looked like a regular—albeit huge—mill from the outside, the interior resembled a mansion. Two staircases greeted him, spiraling up in the shape of a heart. The floors were made of a white, pristine stone. A fireplace stood against the back wall, framed by sculpture crafted out of colored marble. The middle of the mill was hollow, just the stairs wrapping all the way up like the interior of a lighthouse he had seen a few years back, just north of his village. Standing in the center, he looked up and counted five more floors stretched out above him.

Statues of animals and women wearing stone gowns watched Tor as he made his way between the stairs and down the hall.

"Lightning, isn't it?"

Tor whipped around, heart in his throat.

Engle stood there, a jar of vegetables in his hand. "It's still good," he said with a shrug. Tor followed his friend into a kitchen larger than the one in his father's restaurant.

Lest he be accused of slacking off on his responsibilities, Engle puffed up his chest proudly. "Found plenty of beds upstairs, with the softest blankets you've ever felt. I want to take some home with me." Tor didn't have the heart or energy to tell his friend that they would certainly not be hauling a comforter on their backs all the way to the Night Witch. "There's water, too, though not much."

"That's fine," Tor said. "I found some at the pub."

Something behind Engle's head caught Tor's attention. It was a painting, crafted out of swirling, oily strokes. He walked over to it, then pressed a hand against its expertly cut frame.

There was a family: a mother, father, and two small children—all wearing brightly colored clothing and smiling. They were beautiful, especially the woman, whose shining

ALEX ASTER

brown hair seemed soft as silk, her eyes the green of emeralds. Tor squinted. "Something happened here," he said. Perhaps he was wrong. Maybe the village's inhabitants hadn't simply up and left.

"What do you mean?"

"Look around. This place wasn't always so dark."

By the time they made it back to Melda, she had sweat on her brow and had almost completed a sweater. "Lucky enough, I found a thicker fabric in the back room. Saved me hours of work, since now I don't have to line them with wool..." She looked up from her station. "How did you fare? Any food?"

Engle grinned. "Plenty. Well hidden, though."

They ate dinner in the mill kitchen, using spoons they found in drawers to scrape jars that held corn and other vegetables. This was good. They couldn't just live on bread alone. They needed to get their strength back if they were going to face the witch.

Melda agreed the townspeople had clearly fled something bad enough to make them up and leave their entire lives behind, valuables and all. She assured them, however, that whatever the villagers had run away from must have been long gone.

Tor hoped she was right.

Using a box of matches Engle had discovered in a cabinet,

248

they lit a fire that warmed Tor to the bone, then made their way to the second floor. Each person had their own room. Tor's had an enchanted dragon clock that breathed fire when it was time to wake up; he guessed it had belonged to the family's son, once upon a time.

Though he finally had a comfortable bed for the first time in days—complete with dust-covered pillows, sheets, and a wool-lined blanket—Tor still found he couldn't sleep. Thoughts tossed and turned in his brain like a poorly built ship in a hurricane. Not so much thoughts...but fears.

Tor feared failure.

It was the reason he had always hated his leadership emblem and why he had never tried to do well in school. His mother was one of the best Chieftesses of the last century—how could he ever compare?

So instead of trying and failing to live up to her impossible standards, Tor convinced himself he didn't *like* leadership and had been gifted the wrong marking. Unfortunately, he was beginning to understand that might not be it at all.

Maybe he *had* been given the right emblem—but had been too afraid of failing to use it.

Perhaps it was the Shadows and the dark effect it had on minds, but Tor stayed wide awake for hours. His fears turned into worries, and those worries bloomed into guilt. It was an endless cycle that made him feel as though his entire body had turned into a swirling black hole.

He refused to kill the witch—which meant he needed to somehow *convince* her to end the curse.

And he didn't have the slightest idea of how he might do that.

In the middle of reprimanding himself for not being able to fall asleep, he heard a creak. The soft groan of wood being stepped on in the middle of the night.

He stood and lit the candle on his bedside table. If Melda was awake, maybe there was work to be done. He would do anything to help if it meant not having to be alone with his torturous thoughts.

Sure enough, when Tor opened his door, Melda was there, dressed in a nightgown she had likely found in one of the wardrobes. She turned to him, wide-eyed. "Did you hear that?" she whispered.

He squinted at her. "That wasn't you?"

She shook her head.

They quietly made their way to Engle's room. He was splayed out on the bed like a silver falcon in flight, clearly having no trouble sleeping. Tor woke him up with a sharp poke in the arm. With an annoyed grunt, he followed them back down the hall, still half asleep.

In the dark of night, they walked to the middle of the second floor and craned their heads to look up at the levels above. There, at the very top, they saw a light.

Melda turned to face them, eyes wide and solemn. "Someone else is here."

●)) (

They walked up the spiral steps, Tor gripping his candlestick tightly with both hands in case he had to use it as a weapon. Engle had woken up completely now and was at the rear, teeth chattering as if he expected a phantom to appear at any moment.

Melda led the way, closely followed by Tor. He stepped as quietly as possible, strategically: heel first, then arch, then toes, evenly distributing his weight. Engle's foot landed on a loose floorboard, and the wood groaned loudly, echoing through the mill.

Tor froze, Melda gasped. A few moments ticked by without anything, and Tor breathed out a sigh of relief.

A voice rang through the house. "I know you're coming."

Melda bit at her knuckle. Tor balanced between wanting to run out of the house at full speed and satisfying his curiosity about who had spoken.

"Let's go," Engle said, already heading toward the first floor.

Melda and Tor said, "No," at the same time.

Engle scowled.

They continued upward, not bothering to muffle their steps anymore. When they reached a doorway coated in light, Tor held his candlestick out in front of him, the way he might a sword. They burst inside.

An old woman sat in the corner of the room, enveloped by an enormous armchair. Her body looked like a bag of bones in her loose nightgown, her face sunken down as if her skin had encountered quicksand. Her hair looked like a sickly white bird perched atop her head. She was hunched into a C shape, shoulders at her ears.

"Who are you?" Melda asked.

The woman's mouth turned into a smile. She was missing most of her teeth—the rest were rotten. "Who am I?" she said. "I am the woman of this house."

Tor remembered the painting downstairs. "*You're* the one in the painting?" he asked, not concealing his surprise.

She nodded.

Engle, who had seen the beautiful woman in the portrait, twisted his face as if he had just smelled something foul. "How long ago was that?"

"Five years, give or take."

Surely she was confused. If they truly were the same person, then it must have been painted at least *fifty* years before—not five.

The woman knocked her remaining teeth together, making a vile cracking noise. "I sense your disbelief. Let me tell you what happened."

She motioned for them to sit, and they did.

"Our village wasn't always in the Shadows. We always lived *near* it, but not *in* it. My husband was the biggest maker of flour in all of Emblem Island. We had parties in the Mill, I wore beautiful gowns made of spider silk." It was hard for Tor to imagine the tiny, hollowed-out woman at a ball. "My life was perfect," she said, her voice shaking. "Until it wasn't."

"What happened?" Melda asked slowly, her voice soft and encouraging.

"One day, the sun went dark. Ash fell from the sky, like wicked snow. It fell on everything—our houses, our clothes. Little pieces of evil. We should have known what was coming. But our lives were good. No one wanted to leave. So we stayed.

"The next day, I left to get paper at the market. A man was

standing in the middle of the town square, covered in thick, dark plaster. It had fallen out of nowhere. He reached toward me, then hardened, one hand outstretched. That afternoon, the sun disappeared and darkness came—it killed our cattle, demolished our crops, poisoned our water. And it kept us from getting help. No one who left the village ever returned.

"In the dark, people turned on one another. Neighbor against neighbor, fighting not for shoes or books or even dobbles, but *food*. Water. It turned us into our darkest selves. We watched everyone we had ever known drop dead over the course of just a few weeks. And who else to blame but the witch? Her darkness, it's growing. Eating villages up whole."

"How did you survive?" Tor asked. He remembered the water at the bar and the food in the kitchen. The old woman must have gathered those recently. But how? And from where?

She laughed then. "Survive? Do you call *this* surviving?" She pointed a skeletal finger at her sagging face. "Living through darkness hardened my heart, stripped me of life. I should have died."

Melda walked over and placed her hand over the woman's. "Where are your children?" she asked gently. She had seen the same painting Tor had, with the two smiling kids—one blond, the other a redhead.

The old woman blinked up at her, eyes sunken down into

her face. For a moment, Tor thought she might cry. Then, she smiled.

"I ate them."

Melda jumped back, hand placed over her heart. "You what?"

"Them, and every other villager left. *That's* how I survived. It had its price, of course." She pointed at her face once more in explanation.

For a moment, they were frozen in place.

Then they slowly backed out of the room and closed the door behind them. As much as Tor wanted to run screaming into the night and leave the mill far behind them, he knew they needed to stay. Melda had to finish their warm clothes. They would probably perish if they attempted to venture deeper into the Shadows without adequate supplies.

"It's not as if she can outrun us or something," Melda reasoned. "If she tries something, I can't imagine we'd have much trouble stopping her."

Tor shook his head. "I don't know. Did you get a look at her emblem?" If it was a warrior mark, the old woman might be more capable at killing them than she had looked.

She nodded, wincing. "I did, actually."

"Well?" Engle looked at her expectantly. "What was it?"

Melda shuddered, her face a peculiar tint of green.

"Cooking," she said.

The Army of Bones

Once upon a drop of blood, there was a poisoned lake. It was as large as a small sea and smelled of bile and death. Long ago, before it was a lake, it had been a sacred burial ground. Then, the Night Witch flooded its soil, and the bones slipped from the dirt into her gray, putrid water.

With a curl of her finger, the Night Witch commanded the bones to come together, forming beings made up of parts from several different long-gone souls. They made angry, vicious creatures who craved what they did not have—flesh. And their own bones back, so they could be whole once more. The monsters laid at the bottom of the lake, waiting for any hint of life to pass. For only a taste of the living offered any comfort.

Years went by without a kill. The bones stayed submerged for so long, a layer of algae grew over and around them; a flesh of sorts. It made them stronger.

It is said that should a person manage to remove a single bone from the lake, they would be able to brew a potion for unparalleled strength. It is also said that should they fail, the beasts would tear them to pieces, the same way they were once separated from their parts.

The Night Witch alone controls these bonesulkers. To this day, they await her command from the lake's depths, an army submerged in the shadows.

17

ROTTEN

The next morning, Tor heard the old woman scurrying down the stairs faster than seemed possible given her thin, crooked legs. He hadn't slept a wink after hearing her story, even with his door locked.

A spread of breakfast waited for them in the kitchen. Melda and Tor exchanged horrified looks, not wanting to eat anything the old woman had cooked. But their stomachs growled right along with Engle's, who didn't seem too bothered by eating food served by a professed child-eater. Besides, there was no one left for the old woman to cook up.

To their knowledge, at least.

The woman cheerfully explained that after the darkness had passed, she had found a hidden food store and a well with drinkable water. After seasons of trying, her land became fertile enough to yield vegetables, though they tasted a bit sour, and a few weeks prior, a traveler who needed a room had in exchange given her his, which provided her with more than enough milk.

It was at the end of this explanation that Engle cried out.

Melda jumped up. "What is it?"

Engle said nothing, but pointed at his curse. Melda paled.

Dark lines had started to sprout out of the dark lips on his wrist, all the way down his forearm, resembling tree roots. It took Tor a moment to realize that those black lines were Engle's veins.

"This isn't good," he said, shaking his head. "Not good at all."

Engle cradled his arm.

"Curses are leeches." Melda spoke slowly and softly, like the tone of her voice could make the meaning of her words less frightening. "They suck the life out of their host. Not immediately, but, it's been days now..."

Melda's curse had only produced a few tiny lines. Tor's looked similar to hers. Only Engle had truly started to rot.

They had decided to call it *rotting,* because that sounded slightly better than *dying.*

They planned to leave after breakfast, but a storm rolled in while they ate. Wind howled outside, window shutters clapped against the glass in frightening smacks. Dark clouds circled like a pack of wolves, trapping them in the mill for the time being.

"Go out there, and the forest will eat you right up," the old woman said. And though her word choice made Tor's breakfast threaten to come back up, she was right. Leaving before the weather improved would be a mistake.

He looked over at Engle and found him draped over his plate, eyes barely opened. Melda screamed, and they helped him up to his room. In minutes, the curse had spread all the way to his shoulder.

While Engle rested and the dark clouds broke open, Tor spent hours reading the remaining stories, trying to find any clue about where they needed to go next. Trying to read between the lines. He even studied "The Sun and Moon," though it wasn't technically a monster myth. And, even though "The Army of Bones" was the most helpful, it was useless, since the map didn't show a body of water nearby. It didn't show *anything* in the Shadows. Desperate, he asked the old woman if there was a lake nearby, but she ignored him, humming as she dusted the same set of yellowed china, over and over. By the end of the afternoon, he had shoved *The Book of Cuentos* back into his backpack without making any progress.

He went to check up on Engle and found him breathing peacefully, though his curse had crept up to his neck. Not wanting to leave in case Engle's condition worsened even more, Tor sat on the floor and ended up falling asleep against the bed frame.

When he awoke, the room was plunged in darkness. He blinked once, twice, then jumped up. Part of his mind feared something horrible had happened while he had slept—like that the curse had rotted his friend all over...or, worse, that the old woman had baked Engle into a biscuit.

One look at the bed calmed Tor's crazed thoughts. Engle was fine. Or, at least, as fine as he could be, given the circumstances.

He slipped out of the room, then knocked on Melda's door. No response. He guessed at what that meant and made his way downstairs, then outside. The wind and rain had stopped, but the ground was slippery with mud.

At night, the town looked even eerier, the ash-coated buildings hard to see. He walked with his hands out in front of him, feeling around until his eyes adjusted. Even the moon seemed to be shining elsewhere, but candlelight illuminated the clothing shop, helping guide his way. Tor spotted Melda through the window; she was hunched over as she sewed their outfits with the speed of an expert. When he opened the door, she jumped.

Her hand was over her heart. "You scared me," she said. The fear melted from her face, leaving only surprise. "What are you doing here?"

He sat on the stool beside her. "I'm here to help."

"Okay," she said, still looking suspicious. Then she shrugged. "Well, I actually need to get your measurements anyway. I guessed for some of them, but the clothing's useless if it doesn't fit right."

Melda unfurled a tape measure she must have found in the shop. Tor stood with his arms out as she quickly took the measurements, then wrote them down.

"Melda?"

"Yes?"

"I—I wanted to..."

She looked up at him, blue eyes impatient. "Yes?" she repeated.

He sighed. "I wanted to apologize."

She blinked too many times, then looked down. "What for?"

"I'm sorry I left. I'm sorry you and Engle got dragged into all of this. I'm sorry I put our lives in danger. Engle is up there, *dying*, and it's all my fault." He heard his voice crack and locked his jaw.

Melda put the tape measure down. "It's okay," she said. "We all make mistakes. It's not like you *made* us touch the curse. It's my fault for butting in." She shook her head. "I always do that."

"No," Tor said quickly. "Melda, if you hadn't butted in, I wouldn't have had any chance at getting rid of the curse. *You're* the one who led us to the know-all in the first place."

She shrugged. "I guess." There was a moment of quiet. Then, she took a deep breath. "I'm sorry, too."

His eyebrows pulled together. "For what?"

"The way I acted in class. I always made a point to be the best. To make sure Mrs. Alma thought so. Even after you were nice enough to give me your books... I shouldn't have done that."

Tor blinked, taken aback. "Why?"

She breathed out roughly, then twirled her necklace between her fingers. Tor had noticed that she did that when she was nervous. He had watched her do it for years in class, without knowing what the blue pendant held. "I'm sorry if I ever made you feel bad. I just—I can't afford not to do well. I guess I thought I *had* to be better than you. I mean, your mom's the Chieftess! How can I compete with that?"

"Not everything's a competition, Melda."

She squinted her eyes at him. Not in a mean way, but pensively. "Isn't it, though? I *need* to graduate at the top of our class so I can get a great position. Maybe even outside of Estrelle, if the pay is better, so I can help my family." Her bottom lip trembled, just a little. "My dad, he hurt his back. Who knows how much longer he'll be able to work in the mines? And when he can't, I'm all my family has."

Tor felt terrible. He had never had to worry about his family, beyond making sure they didn't find out about his swimming. His biggest stressor in life was that he didn't like his emblem. That worry seemed insignificant compared to Melda's. He didn't know what to say. He wished he could help her...

"What if I suggest a new policy to my mom?" Tor said. Melda wiped a tear from her cheek. "Something to help with the cost of your brothers' medicine or to change your dad's job?"

Her eyes softened. "You would do that?"

"Of course," he said. He added nervously, "That is, if I ever see her again."

Melda surprised him by smiling. "You *will*, Tor. We're not going down without a fight." She used one of her many ribbons to tie back her hair. After nearly a week without seeing a brush, her loose curls had turned into mostly knots. Before she got back to work, she looked at him again. "Which emblem did you wish for?" she asked. "On Eve."

Tor remembered the judgment in Melda's eyes when he

revealed he'd wished to be rid of his leadership marking. But a lot had happened between then and now. He sensed that this time she would respond more empathetically. "Water-breathing," he said quietly.

She nodded, looking down at her fabrics. "Makes sense."

Tor looked surprised.

"Your hair, in class." Melda shrugged. "It's always wet. And there's always sand on your clothes." She passed him a needle and thread. He followed her sewing movements.

Together, they worked to the whisper of wind hissing through a broken window in the shop, staying up until all three outfits were ready.

● ☽ ☽ ☾

Engle groaned as Tor and Melda entered his room. The curse had traveled to the other arm overnight. It was a ghastly sight, the dark lines tracing where light blue veins typically sat. "How does it look?" he croaked, eyes still closed.

"Not bad," Tor said, trying not to choke on the lie.

Melda's mouth hung open in horror, and Tor signaled for her to pull herself together, in case Engle opened his eyes and saw the truth written all over her face. She quickly composed herself. "How are you feeling?"

"Like I died two days ago."

"Oh, okay," she said, smiling. "If you're already dead, then I guess you won't want to see our new outfits..."

He opened his eyes so forcefully it seemed he could see right through the door Melda had hidden their newly made clothing behind. Engle broke into a wide grin. "They look amazing!" he said. Melda took the hanger off the door's hook, then presented it to him. There were four pieces: pants, a sweater, socks, and a cape that looked almost like a coat, but without sleeves.

"I had some help," Melda said, shooting a small smile in Tor's direction. Then, her expression became serious again. "Anyway, we need to leave today." She spread out the map on the end of Engle's bed.

Engle blinked. "But we don't know where we're going."

He was right. And searching the Shadows blindly could take days.

Days they didn't have.

"I know," Melda said. "But we aren't going to find her sitting here. With any luck, we'll happen upon the lake from 'The Army of Bones.' From there, her castle should be really close by." Though she sounded optimistic, Tor saw right through her hopeful tone. She was just as worried about Engle as he was.

Tor closed his eyes for a few seconds too long before

opening them. He was exhausted. Unsteady. His own curse had begun spreading its way up his arm, carving a trail of burning pain.

He left the room with his new outfit, a knot of anger in his chest. They had gone all this way, figured out all of those tales, for what? To still not have the slightest idea where in the Shadows the Night Witch lived? To possibly die before finding her?

This was his doing, he reminded himself. He and his stupid wish were the reasons why his best friend was in the other room, rotting.

It was all his fault.

Tor kicked the foot of his bed, and the headboard slammed against the wall satisfyingly. His toe throbbed, but he turned and kicked something else—his backpack.

All of its contents went flying, including *The Book of Cuentos*, which slid across the floor, stopping only when it reached the dresser. One of the glass trinkets fell off its top and cracked into a thousand pieces.

Tor sunk to the ground, hands running through his hair. He choked out something between a growl and a sob.

And that was when he saw it. Not *saw*, really, because he had seen it countless times before. But this is when he truly noticed it—

A small, silver symbol on the spine of the storybook: a

key. Not just any key though; he had seen this *same* marking before...

But where?

"Melda!" Tor yelled, running out of the room. "I got it!"

● ☽ ☽ ☾

Tor opened the map so forcefully, it ripped at the very top. He pointed to the symbol on *The Book of Cuentos*'s spine, then at a place in the large black hole that was the Shadows.

Nothing important sat there—or so they had thought. Just the map's legend, indicating which symbols represented geographical features, like mountains, woods, or rivers. The same one Melda had used to find Willow Wood.

He pointed at a drawing of a key, positioned right next to the words "Map Key."

"This isn't part of the map's legend, it's a *place* on the map," he said, talking so quickly he wondered if his friends could understand him. "It's a *place*, Melda. Look, the symbols are exactly the same."

Melda and Engle looked at the legend, then at the book's cover, and nodded, but said nothing.

Tor threw his arms over his head, exasperated. "Do you know what this means?"

Engle sighed. "To be honest—no."

Tor rolled his eyes and pointed at the book's spine yet again. "I'm willing to bet *this symbol* represents the person we've been following this entire time, the only person who met the Night Witch and survived. The *storyteller*." He motioned toward the map. "And *this* is where they live."

Engle nodded. "All right, I get it. That key is their family crest or something, and now you've discovered it's on the map, somewhere in the Shadows. But what good does that do us? This book is ancient, Tor, my own grandmother read it as a child. The storyteller's dead."

Engle had a point. "I know. But maybe he has family who still lives there." He motioned toward the key on the map. "People who might know how he managed to escape the Night Witch without dying. And—even better—maybe they know where to find her." He turned to Melda. "I know it sounds absurd, but it's a better bet than wandering around, hoping we'll stumble upon the Night Witch's lair. They might be able to lead us right to her!"

"I don't know..."

He breathed out roughly. "Please, Melda. I know this is risky, and I might be completely wrong. And I know that I'm the one who got us into this mess in the first place." Tor put a hand on her shoulder. "But please, trust me."

Melda looked down at the map, deep in thought. Her gaze soon drifted over to Engle's arm.

With a shaky breath, she nodded.

Tor rushed back to his room to put on his new clothing. After he pulled on the pants, sweater, and cape, he stood in front of the full-length mirror, studying himself.

It was not the clothes he looked at, though they were lovely. He saw the eye on his forearm, and the tiny black lines growing underneath it. He saw a bare wrist. One that, for his entire life, had worn two purple rings.

He remembered his excitement at throwing his wish into the bonfire during Eve. Looking back, it was easy to see how wrong he was. Someone who had been born with everything— and had thrown it all away.

But that wasn't completely true.

Even now, Tor could not bring himself to apologize for not liking his leadership classes or having another passion. What he *did* feel sorry for was letting his hatred of his mark overwhelm every other part of his life.

On Eve, Tor's world had been small. He had not known hunger. Or struggle. Or true life-or-death fear.

Standing there, in a town that had been wiped clean of its inhabitants, emblems seemed almost insignificant. Unimportant. All Tor wanted was to be rid of the curse and to go home. He didn't even care whether or not he completed his Grail, as long as his friends were safe.

He turned away without gazing at his face. He did not have to see it to know he wore the expression of someone deeply afraid... A person about to venture into a lion's den. Even if they managed to find the storyteller's descendants, and then the Night Witch, Tor did not know how he, a markless twelve-year-old, was supposed to convince a creature that lived in storybooks, nightmares, and shadows to reverse their curse.

But he would try.

The Faceless Man

Once upon a puddle of stars, a man was walking through a forest and happened upon a stream. He glanced down, only to see his reflection for the first time.

"I'm divine," he said.

Now that he knew how handsome he was, he demanded to be married to someone equally as beautiful. He searched far and wide, in villages big and small. Before he knew it, he had searched them all. Yet, he found fault in every face except his own.

So, he kept looking, until he found himself back in the forest in which he had started. There, he happened upon a woman, sitting near a river. Her skin was bright gold, her hair a starlight woven silver.

"At last!" he yelled. "A person to match my splendor!"

At that, the woman laughed. She said, "Fool, for my hand, you are no contender."

He startled. "But my face is perfect. The best you'll ever find."

She shook her head and said, "I see not your face, but your soul, and it is rotten. You are self-absorbed, critical, and vain." The woman sighed. "I bet your favorite word is your own name."

She dipped her golden hand into the water.

"I curse you to wear every other man's face." And just like that, his features were erased.

He became a shadow, without a mouth, eyes, or nose. A shape-shifting creature destined to hide in the darkness, waiting for another face to steal and add to his collection.

That is how the first vanor came to be.

A man punished for his own vanity.

18

THE STORYTELLER

The old woman waved them out of the house in a dusty old gown. "Good luck!" she screamed, swinging a dirty handkerchief through the air, though she had absolutely no idea where they were going. The storm had cleared overnight, and Tor took it as a good sign.

There was no evidence of life in the forest beyond the town, not a breath of wind or a single scurrying creature, but Tor didn't mind—for the silence meant they were getting closer. They walked for miles, Melda looking between the compass and map. With Engle rotting away, they had little room for error.

Back at the mill, Melda had found the flowers she had collected near Cristal Town. Though wilted, they still wore their pastel shades. She wove the stems into a bracelet and tied it around her wrist...a reminder of the colorful world that waited for them, far, far away.

But even with the flowers, the Shadows was a gloomy place. Tor felt covered in soot, though nothing fell from the sky. His feet dragged, heavier than ever, like he was trying to walk through water. He waved his arms in front of him, wondering if they were wrapped in some sort of transparent yet tangible smog he could not see. But his fingers encountered nothing.

He shivered, a chill crawling down his spine. There was something eerie about not being able to physically feel malice in the air...like hearing a whisper and turning around to see no one there.

"We're getting close," Melda said after a couple of hours, her voice full of relief. Not a moment too soon, either. Engle's curse had slowed him down; every step looked like it took great effort. Tor handed him the bag of food, and watched Engle take small bites of cheese the old woman had gifted them. No one needed it more than he did.

Tor looked over Melda's shoulder. Before leaving, they had tried their best to put locations in the Shadows on the map, determining distances based on other places they'd traveled. It had taken them roughly the same time to walk from Garth to Willow Wood as it had the tower to the mill, so they used their fingers to measure the distances and added both stops to the parchment.

According to their markings, the key symbol was southeast of the mill, halfway into the Shadows.

But what if their guesses were wrong? They didn't have watches. And time on this side of Emblem Island seemed to move differently.

"If this house exists, it should be right up ahead," Melda whispered.

Tor cracked his knuckles in anticipation. He knew he was right about this, about the storyteller's residence. He had to be. And even if the author's house was abandoned, at the very least it would offer some sort of haven from the dark, thick atmosphere, and a place for Engle to rest.

His friend looked ahead, eyes half closed. His expression was blank. Was there nothing for miles?

Was Tor wrong?

Doubts raided his head and fear froze in his chest. He came to a stop.

If he was wrong, they would have wasted the very last bit of their lifelines traveling to a place that didn't exist. They would be stuck in the center of the Shadows, walking blindly. How long would Engle last that way?

Tor did something he had been avoiding. He looked down

at his palm. The brightest part of the rainbow lines was the very end. They didn't have days anymore.

They had hours.

Had Tor wasted theirs?

"Tor," Engle croaked from up ahead. He ran forward to meet him—

—and froze. The trees ended abruptly at a pair of gates made of twisting metal. They formed a familiar symbol—the same key from the spine of *The Book of Cuentos*.

Tor exhaled deeply.

He really was right. He had figured it out, without anyone's help.

They still had a chance.

Melda pushed at the gates gently, with a single finger, and they swung open with a creak loud enough to wake the dead.

If anyone *was* home, they certainly knew they had company.

Beyond the gates sat a long, winding path, and behind that, a house large enough to be described as a palace. It was crafted out of dark brick, with Gothic, pointed windows, the shimmer of stained glass within them.

Tor squinted. He could have sworn he saw the glass *move*.

No, he shook his head. It must have been a trick of the light.

The front door stood as tall as the one in Aurelia's castle, though this one had no handle. It didn't even have so much as a knocker.

Tor pounded his fist against the wood, but it barely made a sound, and soon his knuckles were raw.

Engle stepped up to give it a try, just as the entryway flung open.

A small boy with large, blinking eyes and hair dark as night stood there. He looked frozen for a moment, startled, then turned and ran down the hallway.

Melda and Tor looked at each other, wondering what to do next. He shrugged and followed the boy inside. Now that they knew someone lived there, Tor was not about to turn away just because they were technically uninvited.

The ceilings reached fifty feet high, crafted out of shining obsidian. The floors were a gray granite that seemed to change color based on the angle of light shining down. These were rare, expensive materials, hardly ever used in making residences that did not belong to a queen or ruler.

But it was the *walls* Tor stopped to stare at.

On either side of the hall hung dozens of large, expertly woven pieces of fabric.

"Storytelling tapestries," Tor whispered in awe. They were precious, extremely hard to make—hanging only in the nicest of libraries or homes. A village was lucky to have *one* in its collection, yet this house had fifty.

Tor stood beneath one that featured a snake with a head at each end. It slithered around the textile, hissing on its way, until the story started over again, with a young, happy couple who had just gotten married.

"'The Hydroclops,'" Melda said from somewhere behind him. "The first monster myth."

The next tapestry held a ship stopped in a glimmering sea, a beautiful face waiting among the waves. She floated with grace, and turned to look right at Tor with purple gem eyes, smiling wickedly. He kept walking, passing by a giant eating a man in a single gulp, then a woman crying into a river. Then, a girl with silver hair and a boy who looked entirely gold, reaching to touch hands—but never meeting. The rest of the books' stories followed, played out on the pieces of fabric in vibrant colors.

When the tales were done, each of the stories began anew.

"Who are you?" An angry voice sounded down the hall. Tor turned around. The little boy was gone, an older man having taken his place. "What are you doing in my house?"

Melda stepped forward. "We were let in by what must be

your grandson." She cleared her throat. "We were hoping to speak with you."

The old man did not move an inch. "Be that as it may, I have no interest in speaking with *you*. Now, get out."

"But—"

"Out!"

No. They didn't get this far to turn back now. "We have traveled for a week, across the worst of Emblem Island. We have risked *everything* to find the Night Witch." Tor took a step closer to the old man, chin high. "I'm going to put an end to her darkness."

The man's hunched-over body went still. There was silence.

Then, he began to laugh, the sound echoing through the hall. "Oh, really? Because I bet you don't even know where she is." He glared at Tor. "I bet that's why you're here."

"What is this guy, a know-all?" Engle groaned.

"No," the man responded. "I just know a blustering fool when I see one. So determined to find something, you don't stop to think of what you'll do when it's right in front of you." His jaw locked. "Just like my great-great-uncle."

Melda stepped forward. "The storyteller?"

The man nodded sharply.

"But he found the witch," Melda continued. "He lived. He *wrote* about her."

The man barked out another laugh, this one full of spit. "And got himself killed for it!" All at once, his expression became serious. He looked to the floor, grimacing. "Got us all cursed." That was when Tor noticed the marking on the man's neck, an eye just like the one he had on his arm.

Tor pulled up his sleeve. "I don't know what yours did to you, but our curse shortened our lifeline." He cleared his throat, trying to steady his voice. "I will not stop until I find her, I promise you. And when I do, I *will* make her put an end to this. You'll be rid of your curse, we all will." He swallowed. "But to do that, you need to help us."

The man lifted a hand and pressed a single finger against the eye on his neck. At that moment, the little boy scurried back into the hallway, and Tor saw he had the same marking on his own skin. He rushed to hug his grandfather's leg, and the old man sighed, the sound full of foggy sorrow.

Then, he nodded.

●)) (

"My name is Etler Key." They sat at a dining table that was big enough to fit twelve people, drinking tea that tasted of sunflower seeds and warmed Tor to the bone. It seemed to be helping Engle, who was already on his third cup. "My

281

great-great-uncle, Vero Key, was an explorer. He sought to see every wonder that inhabited Emblem Island in order to document it in his journal. He started west, then traveled all the way toward home, encountering various...*creatures* on his way. The last stop, he said, would be the very edge of the island, where the Night Witch was rumored to live.

"And he *did* make it there...but exactly what he encountered, no one knows for certain."

"What do you mean?" Melda said. "Her description is in the book, it's the last story."

Etler continued as if she had not said a word. "When he returned home, it was as a different man. He spent months alone in his study, writing stories based on the monsters he had seen, crafting them into a book. Rarely spoke a word about the witch, except for the ones he wrote. He had been cursed to forget practically everything, besides what he included in *The Book of Cuentos*, and her location. That, he wrote on a map and was insistent that every generation memorize it. Why, I do not know. But that same curse weakened him until he died just a handful of years later.

"The curse survived. A variation of it has been passed down his bloodline, leaving his descendants unable to leave this house...why? So that we can never tell a soul about the Night Witch's location. Not unless they happen upon us first."

Tor straightened. "So you *do* know where she is?" he asked, eyes wide in excitement.

The old man groaned, then slammed his fists against the table, making his silverware jump. "Did you not hear a word I said? If you try to find the Night Witch, she will never let you live—not if you've seen her true form. She will kill or curse you further, just as she did Vero!"

Etler was right, of course. If his story was true, then the Night Witch had gone to great lengths to keep her location a secret. She would no doubt eliminate any threat to that, Tor knew.

"I'm willing to take that risk," he said, sounding more confident than he felt. What other choice did he have? His lifeline had been reduced to a tiny stub. It was too late to turn back, even if he wanted to. He could only go forward.

The old man nodded, solemn. He had a gleam of something in his eye—maybe respect, perhaps hope. Before Tor could figure it out, that glimmer vanished. "Walk east until the dirt turns black. Then, travel north until the sky turns gray. Finally, cross the lake. That is where you'll find her."

"Thank you," Tor said, standing from the table.

Etler held his hand up. "There's something else you should know."

THE GOBLIN THIEF

When Estrelle was still living, a goblin happened upon her home. Gray by nature, he wished to have color for himself. While she slept, he dug a sharp nail into her emblem until it drew blood.

Before she could hunt the thief down, he had escaped into the shadows.

Estrelle's emblem contained such concentrated power that the drop of blood gave the goblin a unique gift—the ability to steal color from any source. The green of a tree. The blue of the sea. Yet nothing could change his gray form. He scoured the island, adding every hue imaginable to his collection—a paint box he protected with his life. Still, he was never satisfied. The goblin turned bitter and began stealing color in anger. Just as Estrelle had painted Emblem Island to her liking, he wished to take that color away. He made entire forests shadeless, entire people gray. His stolen ability was passed down to his descendants, who continue to take the color they crave.

19

THE RULES
OF THE GAME

One by one, Melda's veins had started to sour. Tor watched as the dark streaks snaked up her arm like poisoned ink. So far, his had taken the longest to spread, but he knew that in just a few hours, he, too, would be covered in the winding rot of the curse.

But that was the least of his worries. Because in a few hours, he might finally be standing in front of the Night Witch.

Before his stomach could twist with nerves, Tor straightened and took a deep breath. He was prepared.

Finally, he had a plan.

Etler Key knew more than just the Night Witch's location. He knew a secret that could prove to be her weakness.

They traveled east until they came upon a field of black

grass. It was limp, plastered against the ground as if it had been stepped on by giants.

Etler's tea had reinvigorated Engle, he walked easier now. He stopped. Squinted. "There's nothing for miles," he said. "Just...this."

Melda checked the map and shrugged. "This is the way. According to Etler Key, at least."

Tor didn't mind. He preferred nothing to something, because in the Shadows, that something could get them killed. The dirt had officially turned pitch-black, so they turned north, just like Etler Key had instructed.

The air grew as cold as Frostflake, the wind stinging their cheeks in a flurry of icy blasts, and Tor was infinitely grateful for their new clothes. Soon, the chill became almost unbearable and the vaguely blue sky—the only hint of color around—paled into gray.

Walk east until the dirt turns black. Then, travel north until the sky turns gray. Finally, cross the lake. That is where you'll find her.

Tor looked for a lake, the one they had been promised, but saw nothing.

Engle shrugged. "Still nothing else for as far as I can see." He took a deep breath in, closed his eyes. They stayed closed a long moment...and then he doubled over, crying out in pain and gripping his arm. Not the one that held the curse—the other.

Melda ran to him, her hands hovering over his hunched form uselessly, looking around for something, anything that could help. Tor stood very still, mouth ajar, watching as the skin on Engle's arm ripped open like the slow tearing of a seam. In a few horrifying moments, blood spilled over the cape Melda had worked so hard to make, and a clear message appeared, carved deep into his skin: *Don't stop.*

There was a moment of silence.

Then, Melda hooked her arms in each of her friend's and started to run.

"What are you doing?" Engle whispered, his face pale. He had lost a lot of blood.

"It's a rule, I think," she said. "We can't stop moving. No matter what."

"What?"

"Remember what the telecorp told us. He said we would be *tested.*"

Tor swallowed. Melda was right, she must be. She knew what rules looked like better than anyone. And if she was correct...

This was their first test.

Melda was not the best runner. After just a few moments,

Tor noticed that her breathing had predictably turned into wheezing.

She slowed, slipping her arms free.

"Boys?" she said smiling. She wasn't looking at Tor or Engle.

He squinted ahead, but saw no one. Who was she talking about? All at once, a figure appeared, just a few yards away. But it was not a boy.

It was Rosa.

She threw her head back and laughed, two black braids falling behind her. "I knew you'd come back," she said. "I told Mom she was being silly worrying."

Tor said nothing as he neared her. She was there, in the middle of the Shadows, looking exactly as she had the morning they left. Tor wanted nothing more than to hug her, to check her lifeline and make sure it never changed. To hear the melody of her pitch-perfect voice. But when it came time to greet her, Tor ran right past. And Rosa disappeared in a swirl of smoke.

Melda looked like she was about to stop. "What are you doing out here?" she was saying to someone who wasn't there.

Tor hooked her by the arm, so they were locked like they had been before. "No, you don't," he said. He turned to grab Engle, too, but his friend didn't look fazed. He looked weak.

"I saw my parents," he said quietly. "And no way I'm stopping for them."

All at once, the gray clouds above them dropped so swiftly Tor ducked as if the sky was falling down; they stopped a couple of yards off the ground, creating a thick fog. Clouds proved to be cold, frost spun into cotton.

For a few moments, Tor walked on, trying desperately to see through the frigid haze, knowing it was pointless; even Engle was walking blind. Finally he closed his eyes, because somehow the darkness seemed more comforting than the shapeless mist.

A wave of dizziness crashed over him, though all he had done was take a few steps forward—and he wasn't holding on to his friends' arms any longer. The ground beneath his feet felt tilted, and his stomach rose up in response. He wondered if he should slow down, just a little. Maybe stop and get his bearings. He could be running right toward the edge of a cliff for all he knew...

No. The words carved into Engle's arm blazed behind his closed eyelids in memory. *Don't stop.* He hummed a song to reassure himself that not all of his senses were muted. For some reason, he had picked Azulmar Academy's school anthem. A song he had hated for as long as he could remember.

Someone joined in. Somewhere in the endless mist was Melda's voice. Then Engle's. They hummed together, every note permanently burned into their minds since they were six years old.

And Tor didn't feel so lost anymore. He opened his eyes.

Just as their song finished, the clouds dropped again. This time to their ankles. They could suddenly see their surroundings. Tor blinked wildly, and quickly found his friends—Melda to his left and Engle to his right.

Without warning, Engle did the unthinkable. He stopped. Before Tor could yell, his friend slowly held up his arm.

"It's gone," Engle said. "The rule." So they stopped, too.

No one said anything as several seconds ticked by... until, at the same time, they threw their arms around each other.

Engle was shaking from the cold. The color was nearly drained from his face. "My wish," he whispered.

"What?" Tor asked, one of Melda's ribbons almost in his eye.

"My Eve wish. I wanted you both to know it...you know. Just in case."

Tor wanted to tell Engle to keep his wish to himself, that they would be fine. But he couldn't promise that. So instead he said, "What was it?"

"I wished for adventure," Engle said. "So it's not just your fault, Tor. I wished for something like this to happen...and I guess it came true."

Melda nestled her head in between Tor and Engle's shoulders. "Whatever happens," she whispered, "it *was* an adventure."

"To adventure," Tor whispered.

Melda and Engle repeated, "To adventure."

And then it was Melda's turn to scream out. She clutched her arm, and loudly ground her back teeth together. A message was being written on top of her hand, below the knuckles.

Three words: *Don't Look Back.*

Tor kept his eyes trained on the fog that rolled in the distance. He told himself that everything was okay, that this was easy even though he heard Melda scream and Engle muttering to himself. He wondered what they were seeing that he could not. He saw nothing, just mist. All he had to do was follow the rules of the game and not turn around.

Tor.

The voice was a whisper in his ear, as if someone was standing right next to him.

Chills spread down his arm, but he gave no answer.

Tor, the voice repeated. *You're going to wish you were dead.*

His chest froze. "Why?"

You're going to be gifted the greatest gift of all.

His eyebrows came together. He was going to wish he was dead, but was also going to be gifted the greatest gift of all? Which was it?

I'll give you a choice. Turn around, and I'll make all of your dreams come true. I'll give you the emblem that would complete you. The one that would delight you.

He bit the inside of his mouth. "In exchange for what?"

Your friend.

Tor immediately shook his head no.

Don't you want to know which one?

He shook his head again.

It's the girl. She's the reason you never liked leadership, right? Because from the first day of class, you knew she would always be better? Because Mrs. Alma always called her the best?

Tor swallowed.

It's okay, Tor. Let's get rid of her. We'll do it together. You'll never have to worry about being inferior anymore. You will be the best. Everyone will see that...

Tor winced. The smooth, alluring voice knew what lived

in the darkest part of his heart. It knew things he had been too ashamed to admit.

The voice was right.

You always hated her help, didn't you? Hated that you even needed *help, given who your mother is. It's okay, Tor. Just turn around.*

He shook his head.

Just. Turn. AROUND.

"No!" He yelled the word without a question, without a second's hesitation.

And the voice disappeared.

Tor looked at Melda. The rule on her arm had vanished.

2 0

THE LAKE OF THE LOST

T or prepared himself for the sharp pain, knowing he was
next. He stared down at his arm, waiting. Holding his
breath.

Nothing happened.

So they kept walking.

He took a sip of their remaining water to try to settle
the butterflies in his stomach. But these were some kind of
mutant butterflies, huge and wild, and they danced around
in his belly like dread. The hairs on the back of his neck
prickled as if his body knew before his mind that something
bad was about to happen. Though they were so close to the
Night Witch, a part of him still wanted to turn back. He was
ashamed, but the thought remained, a little fire burning in his
mind.

He knew he was supposed to believe in himself. To have hope. But Tor wasn't naïve. Though he never planned on killing the witch and just wanted to speak to her, the Night Witch likely wouldn't listen. She would attack. And he was a twelve-year-old who had never fought anyone in his life— let alone a Night Witch who had inspired countless legends. She had powers, emblems that could do all sorts of tricks and magic.

Now he had none.

Somehow, thinking those thoughts, negative as they were, comforted Tor. Because if he died, he would die doing something brave. He was going to face the witch, knowing almost for certain that he would lose.

That seemed to Tor like the most noble thing he had ever done.

And also, the most foolish.

"I see something," Engle croaked. "Water."

Tor nodded, remembering Etler Key's directions. Crossing a lake was the very last step. And not just any lake. The lake from "The Army of Bones."

They were so very close.

The fog shifted, drifting around their ankles as they came upon a dock made of creaky wood and covered in barnacles. Tor worried his foot might go right through the planks.

Beyond the sad excuse of a harbor sat a body of water the color of mist. It looked rotten, discolored, a foul scent rising from its surface. A single boat, barely big enough for the three of them, bobbed in the water, tied to the dock by a piece of rope coated in diamond-sharp shells.

"May I interest you in a ride?" The voice was like nails scratched across glass.

A goblin's voice.

Tor stiffened. He had never met one in person, but goblins had a reputation of being greedy, vicious creatures. The being climbed its way onto the dock from the hammock it had been laying on. His skin was the same pale gray as the water, his ears pointed, back hunched over. When he bowed, Tor saw that the nails he extended were coated in dirt, and his garment was falling apart.

"Is that the way to the witch?" Melda pointed across the water. If Tor squinted enough, he could see a cliff, far in the distance. And a castle farther than that.

The creature smiled, his mouth almost reaching his ears. "Yes. She lives just across the Lake of the Lost."

"Then you *can* interest us in a ride."

Engle took a feeble step toward the boat, and the goblin hissed. "Not so fast. Every ride has its price."

Tor's jaw set. "We don't have any money," he said, and it

was true. They had made it this far. A goblin was not about to stand between him and the Night Witch.

The creature laughed, the sound so high-pitched that Tor winced. "I don't want *dobbles*," he said in disgust, as if speaking of trash.

"Then what *do* you want?" Melda asked.

He grinned. "Your eyes."

Melda took a big step back. "What?"

"Just the color."

"Why on earth would you want that?"

The goblin sighed and sprawled out his hands, motioning toward his surroundings. "Look around. It's all gray here," he said. "*Color* is what we crave..."

Tor knew the story. Goblins were the only creatures that could extract color from a being.

"We have other colors that we would happily give you," Tor said, taking a step between Melda and the goblin.

The creature raised a sharp finger. "No, no, no. No negotiations. Once a goblin has spoken its wishes, they cannot be changed."

Melda winced, then took her necklace into her hands.

She presented the pendant to the goblin, her arm trembling, like the act pained her. "Here," she said, voice cracking. "You can have this. It's the same color."

Tor wanted to tell Melda not to hand it to him. That it was far too valuable to give away. He knew how much it meant to her.

But they needed to get across the lake.

The goblin hissed. "What did I just say! Once a goblin has spoken its wishes, they cannot be changed. It is the color of your eyes or nothing!"

"But—"

"*No.*"

Melda bunched her fists and shocked Tor with her next few words. "Very well." She put the pendant back on.

The goblin motioned for Melda to bend down to his height. She then closed her eyes as he placed two long fingers against her lids. She flinched, and Tor flinched along with her.

When Melda opened her eyes again, the beautiful blue color was gone, replaced by a cloudy gray. The change was shocking. He watched as she looked at her reflection in the water, one of her hands immediately finding her mouth.

"It's okay," he whispered to her. "When this is over, you'll drip the blue color from the necklace into your eyes. It'll be like it never happened."

She nodded sharply, mouth closed very tightly, looking as if she wanted to cry...or maybe scream.

Tor turned to the goblin. The blue of Melda's iris was now smeared across his clothing. The creature spun around, admiring himself in the water. Then, he handed Tor two paddles.

"Good luck," the creature called out, as they pushed the boat away from the dock. It was as Tor was paddling that his palm suddenly split open. He gasped in pain, blood puddling at his feet. The third rule was printed there, red as copper: *Don't die.*

●)) (

The boat sloshed from side to side, though the water was quite still. Tor peered over the side, but saw nothing amiss. He turned to ask Engle to look deep into its depths, but saw his friend hunched over, head against his knees.

Tor sat with his back to the cliff, not allowing himself to get a good look at it, or the castle that was getting closer and closer. He gritted his teeth, his arms growing weaker with each push of the paddles against the thick, murky water. His palm was throbbing, but he refused to let them go; doing something was at least a little bit of a distraction from the fear that curled in his stomach like a snake.

Melda pointed a few feet away. "That's a bone, isn't it?"

Long, white, and floating, it was unmistakably a bone.

Engle slowly raised his head and made a gulping noise. "Look," he said, and Melda and Tor craned their heads to get a good view of the water. Bubbles started to pop at the surface, like the lake was boiling.

A flurry of bones followed—dozens, then hundreds, rising in a flash, just as dead fish did in poisoned water. Skulls knocked against the side of the boat.

"It's all right," Melda said, clearly trying to keep calm. "Those are just bones... Bones can't hurt us..."

But Engle did not look worried about the bones. He stared into the lake, eyes wide, and Tor wondered what he could see that they could not. Melda turned to face the direction he was looking, and that was when a head broke the surface—all bone save for the single clump of hair on its scalp. Long, flowing fabric moved behind it in mesmerizing waves as the creature neared the boat.

And then another surfaced. And then another. Until they were surrounded.

A bonesulker thrust its hand out of the lake, toward Engle, reaching for his throat. Its arm was half bone, half algae, two fingers missing altogether.

Before it could reach him, Tor thwacked it on the side of the head with one of his paddles. The beast hissed wildly.

"Go!" Melda said, and he paddled as fast as he could.

But the creatures of the lake were faster. They raced after the boat, screaming, propelling through hundreds of bobbing bones to get to their prey.

One of them broke away—it was longer than the rest, built of twice as many bones. In seconds, it swam ahead of the boat, then turned to press its bone-finger against the starboard. Its strength was enough to stop them completely. Tor's paddles were useless.

They came to a halt.

Nowhere to run, nowhere else to go, they huddled in the middle of the boat. Engle was shaking, and, because Engle's pants were just a little too short, Tor saw that his friend's curse had traveled down to his ankles. He didn't know how Engle was still conscious; the pain must have been unbearable. Tor's arm had just a few streaks, and it burned like the skin there had been carefully peeled back.

"Engle," Melda said, voice shaking. "I want to tell you something. Maybe this isn't the best time, but—I feel like I have to."

He looked at her expectantly.

"I used to think you were just a boy who was always hungry and joking around, but I wanted to say you've been brave. Braver than the rest of us sometimes. Especially on the zippy. And I know we weren't really friends before, and I wasn't kind, but things have changed, and I—"

One of the bonesulkers leapt out of the lake, grabbed Engle by the neck, and pulled him into the ice-cold water. He was gone in an instant.

"No!" Melda screamed, reaching over the boat. Engle's eyes were wide, bubbles exploding from his mouth as they dragged him down. He reached, too, strained to stretch his arms just a little more...

But though their fingers were just inches apart, they did not meet.

She threw herself toward him, but Tor caught her by the waist. Tears in his eyes, he pulled her away.

No.

No, no, no.

He couldn't see his friend anymore, he was—

"Gone," he said, pale as bone. "He's gone."

Tor heard Melda whisper something to herself, words he remembered the giantess saying: "There are many ways to be strong that don't require a sword."

Melda broke free.

She jerked the glass vial from her neck, and shattered it against the side of the boat. A single drop of color fell into the water.

In a flash, the entire lake glowed sapphire blue.

The creatures shrieked, shocked momentarily by the blinding color, their screams muted by the lake's depth. The drop was not enough to change the lake forever.

But it was enough to make the monsters release the boy.

Engle floated up, as if filled with air. His body was very still.

Tor helped Melda haul him into the boat. Engle's eyes remained closed, and large gashes had been sliced through his clothes. He was bleeding, everywhere.

But he was still breathing.

Melda held him close while Tor paddled, tears streaming down her face.

Their boat lurched as the bottom caught on dark, rocky sand. Tor jumped off onto land, then pulled Engle from the boat, laying him on his side. He started to cough up water, then stilled. They needed help—they needed a doctor.

"Go, Tor," Melda said. "Find the Night Witch." She did not have to say to hurry because Engle might not survive the hour. She did not even have to say to be careful or to follow the third rule to a tee. He read it all in her now permanently gray eyes.

With a single nod, Tor grabbed the dagger and headed toward the cliff.

The Night
Witch's Castle

Once upon a full moon, the witch made a lair. A castle to match her wickedness. She crafted it from poison rock, deadly to the touch. She trapped a princess in its foundation, building around her screams, because legend said that was the only way to ensure it would never fall over. Her bones are in the walls.

In this castle on a cliff the Night Witch sits, her skin a sickly gray, speckled with blood-crusted emblems. Words whispered through villages, rumors carried by the wind and down the coast are not enough. For one can only truly know darkness by seeing it for themselves. She is spun from the shadows, a nightmare come to life.

Beware screams at the stroke of midnight. Ravens that fly against the breeze. Storm clouds that appear against a blue sky. Whispers in the wind.

For that is a sign she is near.

2 1

THE NIGHT WITCH

Tor walked across a sandy stretch of land, toward the cliffs and castle that hovered above. His hands were in fists so tight, his nails drew blood. His best friend had almost died. He had *watched* him being dragged down to the depths of a deadly lake. Even now, Engle was clinging to life, sprawled out on a dark beach.

And it was his fault.

It was *her* fault.

He would put a stop to the Night Witch.

The thought was unrelenting, pounding through his mind. He had no fear then, no hesitancy. If he died, then so what? It would be worth it, for Engle, and for Melda. He would do anything to make sure they got out of this alive.

The dagger rocked back and forth in his pocket, poking

him in the thigh, but he did not adjust it. The pain fed his anger, kept it strong.

Right in front of the cliff sat a puddle the size of a well. It was the darkest of blue, spotted with silver specks, like someone had cut out a piece of the nighttime sky and stuck it here.

Get in.

It was the voice from before.

He took off his cape and jumped.

Tor sank like a boulder, traveling what seemed to be a hundred feet deep. It felt good to be in water again, for possibly the last time. Glowing moon-colored crystals lined the smooth sides of the circular tunnel, lighting his way down. Just when the majority of his breath had been released in a stream of bubbles, he reached the bottom.

There was a shadow. It wavered before him, gone, then back again, finally taking shape. If Tor had any breath left, he would have screamed.

The creature had no face, only a flesh-covered canvas where a face should have been. But he wanted one. All vanors did. They lived to steal faces to add to their collections.

And this one wanted Tor's.

It floated, its blankness, along with the ice-cold water, giving Tor chills.

The voice was back again. This time, it said, "*Choose one—and only one. Choose wisely, and you have won.*"

Out of nowhere, three pearls the size of crystal balls appeared, floating in front of the vanor. Tor felt the first jolt in his lungs warning him he'd been submerged for too long.

"Power." The voice was a frosty whisper in his ear as the first pearl glowed purple. Suddenly, the vanor changed into his mother. She floated there, dressed in her ceremonial Chieftess outfit, headpiece and all. *Mom.* Tor reached for her. Then, the creature changed again, into Queen Aurelia, her huge golden dress billowing around her like a balloon.

"Riches," the voice said next, as the second pearl turned gold. The vanor transformed into someone else then, someone Tor had not expected.

Himself.

He saw himself, dressed not in his usual clothes, but in expensive, thick fabrics, large gems sewn onto the pockets. He held a mound of golden dobbles in his hand. His reflection winked at him. Tor couldn't imagine having that much money—enough for anything he could possibly dream of.

Finally, the voice spoke another word. It was sharp like a hiss. "Sacrifice."

The third pearl turned blood red. The vanor stayed as Tor, but the dobbles and gems fell away. He saw himself not winking, but *drowning* until his skin became a horrible shade of blue. Then, the vanor turned into Melda. Her wrist was bare—her curse gone. She was smiling.

Engle was next. Like Melda, his curse had disappeared. He looked healthy—happy.

The voice said three final words. "Choose a pearl."

Was this a trick? A test?

If he chose the third option, would his friends die anyway?

He had been in the water for far too long. Pressure built behind his ribs.

In an absurd way, the feeling was somewhat comforting. It made him remember swimming in the ocean, on a day that felt miles away. So many things had changed.

Including Tor.

His lungs compressed as his body ached for air. He wanted to go home more than he had ever wanted anything in his life. He wished he had been grateful for everything he'd had—everything he had lost.

Then, Tor thought of what he had gained. Two friends he would trust his life with. People he had *survived* with. They were the silver lining of this entire dark mess.

Tor reached for the red pearl and clutched it to his chest.

The orb lit up, illuminating the water like a miniature sun. Tor's body went numb. He couldn't move an inch.

Which meant he couldn't get to the surface.

Something in Tor's throat began to throb and contract, beating like a heart. The need for air became overwhelming.

Like floodgates opening, the first burning gulp of water entered his lungs. It felt like he had swallowed flames, a bonfire lighting in his chest.

I would do anything for the people I love. Tor repeated those words in his mind until they blurred away and he couldn't remember them.

As more and more water shot into his lungs and his eyes started to close, Tor thought about his mother. His father.

Rosa.

As soon as he thought of her, the vanor changed, taking on Rosa's shape and size. His eyes shot open again as his sister floated in front of him, her thick eyebrows twisted in concern. She reached for him, for his hand. He reached out, too. And as soon as their fingers were meant to touch, the vanor turned back into its wicked white form.

Tor's lungs lurched one last time. This was the end. The end of not only his life, but his journey. His quest for the Night Witch. But his friends were safe. They could return without him. And that made it all worth it. He would make the same choice, over and over again, even though dying proved to be slow and painful. He was a moment from the end, he knew.

All at once, the water glowed ice-blue.

And Tor shot to the surface like a shooting star.

He did not stop there. The water propelled him up like a beam of light, hundreds of feet into the air. Tor saw his friends on the beach far below as he flew through the blue shaft at a dizzying speed, until the stream of water finally spit him out. He rolled a few times over jagged rocks before stopping, faceup, in a wide cave.

Tor coughed up water, gasped for air, then coughed some more, his lungs sore and raw. *What happened?* The pain in his head beat fast as a drum. Had he been saved?

With wobbling arms and legs, he finally pushed himself to his feet. And when he turned, he saw something that made him jump back.

A young woman stood in front of him. She had beautiful blond hair and skin that glowed as brightly as bits of sun peeking through clouds.

"I've been expecting you," she said in a voice soft as velvet.

Tor recognized it immediately. He swallowed.

"You're the one who's been helping us," he said. It was *her* voice that had spoken through the mouth on Engle's arm, telling them to jump at the city of Zeal.

She smiled, then nodded.

"Are you a wish-god?"

She had not only helped them on their journey, but also saved him from drowning, just moments before. Maybe he should bow...or at least say thank you.

But then the woman shook her head no.

He froze. "I'm not on a Grail, am I?"

"I'm afraid not."

Her voice had gone deep as the sea, sharp as an icicle. He recognized it, too—it was the same one that had whispered in his ear just moments before, in the tunnel of water. The one that had tempted him, when they'd had to follow the rules.

Half of the woman's hair became the same pitch-black as the curse on his arm. The lace on her dress transformed as well, the velvet so dark it looked wet.

One by one, almost every inch of the woman's body was covered by emblems, little drawings etched into her skin: a skull, a tiger, a chalice, purple flames, a heart, an hourglass, a vial, a silver star. And more still.

Tor swallowed and reached into his pocket for the dagger, clutching it tightly with shaking fingers. "You're the Night Witch," he said. Though covered in markings, she did not look anything like the rotting, grotesque figure the stories had described.

His head was spinning. If the two voices were from the same person, then by helping them, the witch had led them right to her.

She surprised him by laughing.

Why had the witch led him here? Why had she cursed him?

Did any of that really matter?

He swallowed and took a firm step forward. Then, he said, "I know who you really are."

●)) (

For just a moment, the Night Witch froze. Then she walked toward Tor, a wicked smile never leaving her face. "Tell me: What is it that you know?"

"You're the moon," he said. "From the story."

The Night Witch did not say a word.

Etler Key had told them he suspected his great-great-uncle had written "The Sun and the Moon" about himself, after falling in love with a woman he could never be with. The old man believed that love had something to do with their family's curse. And that was when Tor had figured it out.

"You were in love with the storyteller."

The Night Witch turned to look at the cave wall. Spiders crawled along it and out into the gray mist.

Tor's voice was desperate. "You might be a murderer, but there is good in you. The storyteller must have seen it."

"Allow me to tell my own story," she said. "Not to worry. Your friends are fine...for now. But, by the end of this day, one of us will be dead." Her eyes gleamed. "And that, Tor Luna, is a promise."

Tor's jaw locked. He would make sure that Melda and Engle remained safe. This battle was between him and her. And she was absolutely right.

Only one of them would leave the cave alive.

The Night Witch turned to face him. "In a time when emblems were still rare, I was the first to be born with more than one marking: A moon. And a sun.

"The moon gave me the power to kill with a single touch. The sun allowed me to bring a person back to life with the snap of my fingers. A balance, you see. It would have remained so, if not for the event that pushed me into the darkness.

"Word had gotten out that someone in my house had more than one emblem—which they took to mean evil. Too much power. The person was to be imprisoned. The morning the prosecutors were going to make their arrest, my father painted a second emblem onto his skin and hid me in a secret room. They came to the house and saw his markings. Before

I could use my abilities to save him, he was gone. And not just imprisoned. The men who came were not the prosecutors at all, but emblem-thieves. There to take my father's alleged two powers. By killing him.

"Once they realized one of his marks was false, they came back. And found me. But I was ready this time. I killed each one where they stood. My father's emblem became mine, a third one appearing on my skin. I left my house with it, covered in the men's blood, without a single look back. For years, I roamed the island, searching for thieves just like the ones that had killed my father. I killed them before they could end anyone else. And so, my markings grew."

They covered almost every inch of her skin.

Tor gritted his teeth. "You're lying. I know your tale...and that isn't it. It says you killed your father to get his emblem, then left your house covered in his blood. It says you've murdered people—*innocent* people. You're the villain in almost every story."

She smiled, and it was sad. "By design. My story is a lie." The Night Witch looked past him, out of the mouth of the cave. "You are correct, Tor. I loved the storyteller. We loved each other. He was the only one to see the good in me, even after what I had become. But, just like the sun and the moon, we could not be together. The darkness I still harbored put him in danger. So, I made a choice." She swallowed. "I made him forget me—and gave him new memories. Terrible ones. I made him write me into his stories. To make me a monster."

"Why would you ever want that?"

Her eyes became fierce. Angry. She glared at him. "I never *wanted* any of this. But I knew that if I was not made to be fearsome, someone would one day come to slay me." And inherit all of her power, Tor thought. She nodded. "I made him forget everything and cursed his line never to be able to leave their home, because there are those that would capture them in an instant, should they leave my protection of the Shadows. Those that would do anything to hunt me and my power down. They are the only ones who know my location—to share in case someone would one day be worthy of finding me."

She smiled at the horizon. "Alas, Vero remembered something of our love, it seemed, when writing our story. Even my power could not completely erase us from his mind. For years, he fought so hard to remember his stolen memories, it sent him to an early death." She swallowed. "It was a consequence I had not anticipated."

In an instant, her eyes snapped back to his.

"I have spent a thousand years teetering between good and evil. I created the silver falcon. *I* am the wish-god your people speak to on Eve, though I refute that name. I grant those wishes and have enacted many more helpful acts across the island.

"But I am also the mother of the darkness that has eaten up villages. The truth is, Tor Luna, there is someone coming for me and my dark power. One that is not half, but *all* evil. A man who will not rest until he controls the island. I cannot stop him; I have been weakened, and my heart has been tainted, ever since that day they took my father. But yours, foolish as you are, is still intact."

Tor did not know what she meant. Or who she was referring to.

"I saw your wish on Eve. A boy unsatisfied...a blank canvas. Years ago, I blessed a few good Emblemites with a second, or even third emblem, in the hopes they would be the ones to help me destroy the darkness I created, and the host it inhabited. But, pure as their hearts seemed, they were eventually consumed by their power. Darkness ate them up, just as it had me.

"I realized then that what I needed was not several *good* people, but *one* who *didn't want power at all*. So they wouldn't be tempted to exploit it. See, the best leaders are the ones who don't *want* to lead, Tor Luna." She looked at him intently. "When you wished to be rid of your leadership emblem, I knew you were the one I had been looking for. I *led* you here and made sure you didn't die on the journey. Do you really think you could have made it here without my help?"

His chest felt full of tar. So he *had* been cursed for a reason. Not because his wish had been bad—but because it had been useful.

"You passed my test, Tor, by choosing Sacrifice. Now I know you are truly worthy. On Eve you wished for a new emblem, a water-breathing one, and I will give it to you. I will also give you so much more."

He knew now what she meant...what she wanted to give him.

Tor could never be a Wicked, the basis of the word *witch*, a person with multiple markings. Since he was a little boy, he'd learned the evil of having more than one emblem. It was forbidden, a sign of malevolence. His family would become outcasts; his mother could lose everything she had worked so hard for.

"Despite your reluctance, I have made my choice. *You* will inherit all of my power and will replace me in every way. Including in the fight against darkness."

He hadn't wanted to lead a *village*, let alone an entire island against the evil force she was alluding to, whatever it—or he—was. Evil he himself was afraid of.

"Agree to be my heir," she commanded.

"Never," he yelled, pulling out his dagger and pointing it in her direction. He pressed his thumb against the ruby that decorated its hilt as hard as he could, and something strange happened. All at once, the blade shot forward, growing until it became a long, gleaming sword. Then, the entire weapon, from hilt to tip, hardened into a transparent crystal.

It's enchanted. Hope bubbled up in him like liquid in a cauldron. Maybe he still had a chance.

The witch lunged forward, her dress floating behind her, but Tor swung his sword before she could get anywhere near him.

In one quick motion, she raised her hand, and the ground beneath Tor's feet began to shake. It broke open, and dozens of shards of rock like teeth trapped his legs, then torso. The sharp stone tips pierced his clothes, crimson stains blooming through the fabric in blotches.

Tor gathered all of his waning energy and dug the tip of his blade into the ground. The rocks confining him crumbled into powder.

The sword must be able to control the elements. The witch flung her arm out in front of her. From the tip of her finger came a bolt of lightning—long, crackling, and glowing silver.

Tor held the sword parallel to his face, hand outstretched, ready to be fried to a crisp.

And from its blade came a frozen shield that covered his entire body.

The witch's flames crackled against the ice-shield, in glorious orange—but it did not melt. With every burst of fire, the ice grew *stronger*, hardening over and over again until he could barely see in front of him.

The cave went quiet. Tor waited a few more moments, then dropped his aching arms, shield vanishing, sword tip touching the ground. The witch was hunched over, breathing hard.

She had been weakened.

This was his chance. Tor saw her neck—out in the open. Vulnerable. All it would take was two seconds and two steps; a slice through the air, and the Night Witch would be gone.

Tor would be a hero.

He did not move.

The Night Witch began to laugh, the sound echoing through the cave behind them. Tor took a few steps backward as she rose. "I have not seen restraint like this in a while," she said. "Yes, I made a fine choice. Though, even if you *had* wanted to, it's important you know you never stood a chance at killing me." She closed her fist.

And Tor's sword shattered into a million pieces.

The witch took his hand and pressed her thumb right in the middle of his palm before he could pull away. He felt a prick like a bite and winced. The black lines on Tor's arm faded back into the light blue of his veins. The eye on his wrist closed, then shrank, until it too was no more.

"Congratulations, Tor. From now on, you will be the wicked of Emblem Island. New emblems will start to appear very soon. It is up to you to save this island from the shadows. And make no mistake, Tor Luna, darkness has already set its eyes on your village." He watched the witch walk to the edge of the cliff, dress dragging behind her. She turned to look at Tor one last time. "I pray your heart is better than mine." Then, she jumped.

Tor's eyes widened.

Instead of dropping three hundred feet down, the witch's body turned into a dozen birds—half white as snow, half dark as night—and they all flew in different directions.

And Tor felt very numb, knowing what he had become.

The climb down was treacherous, but Tor did not feel an ounce of fear. His worst nightmare had already come true.

His friends waited on the beach. Melda rushed toward him, sand covering her arms, her gray eyes wide and unnerving. "You killed her?" she asked.

"No," he said. "But she's gone anyway." He bent down to where Engle sat. The cuts across his chest made by the bonesulker had been healed. "How are you?"

"I've been better," Engle said. "Luckily, I'm short a pair of lips." He held out his arm for Tor to see.

And Tor tried to smile. He had gotten what he had wanted, after all. His friends were safe, and his Eve wish would be granted. Though not in a way that he could have ever imagined. Not in the way he would have ever wanted.

He should have listened to the legends read to him before bed, the superstitions carried through his village for centuries—he should have heeded the Eve warning and *been careful what he wished for.* Though it was far too late for that now.

"Let's go home," he said. Melda pulled the telecorp's enchanted coin out of her pocket. She held it in a fist, and Tor and Engle put their hands over hers. The token glowed, golden light shining through their fingers, for just a moment.

Before it could work its magic, Melda dropped the coin. It fell onto the sand before Tor picked it up. "What happened?"

Melda didn't respond. Her mouth hung open, choking sounds coming out instead of words.

He turned to see what she was staring at. And when Tor saw a boat with three passengers approaching, he too dropped the coin.

22

HOME

Tor, Engle, and Melda watched as their mothers' boat washed ashore.

Engle looked confused. Tor guessed his friend probably would have never thought his mother would travel a mile for him, let alone across all of Emblem Island. Melda looked relieved.

But Tor was horrified. His mom's normally beautiful, long black hair was completely gray. Like Melda, she had given her color to the goblin. For her son.

Chieftess Luna must have seen the pain written across his face; she took him into her arms. "You're okay, and that's all that matters," she said, tears streaming down her cheeks. She had always been so stoic, calm in the face of every obstacle, big or small. For her to be so emotional now...

"What are you doing here?" he choked out. Along with the gray hair, Chieftess Luna had a deep scratch on her cheek that had already started to scab. There were a few leaves lodged in Melda's mom's curls. Engle's mother limped; she had clearly hurt her leg at some point.

The Chieftess glared at her son. "*You're* the one who leaves home to journey to the edge of Emblem Island, and you have the nerve to ask me what *I'm* doing?"

There, in front of everyone, Tor recounted everything the Night Witch had said. Everything she had *done*.

His was a fate worse than death.

After he finished, his mother held him for a long time and he let her, relief and anger clashing together, water against magma. He had saved them, true. But he would never forgive himself for wishing his Eve wish in the first place. For not having been content with what he had. For risking everything. Because as much as he wanted to blame the Night Witch for what she had made him, he knew the fault was also his own.

They agreed to keep what had happened a secret, until Tor could figure out how to either get rid of—or control—his newfound power. And for that, Tor was grateful.

Then, they stacked their hands over the telecorp's coin, creating a tower-high pile of palms. It glowed gold.

And a moment later, they were gone.

23

ASHORE

A month later, Tor, Engle, and Melda sat on the beach. They met here every morning. It had become their ritual since they returned to Estrelle.

The sky was the pinkish purple of a bruise, the smallest stream of sunlight poking through. Warm ocean water foamed around Melda's outstretched legs. She looked more relaxed, Tor thought, ever since Chieftess Luna had enacted policies that helped families like hers. They had received overwhelming support from the village, allowing Melda's father to get a job in Estrelle, one that didn't hurt his back. With money raised from neighbors, her brothers received a new treatment for howling cough from a healer in Zeal. Now that they could finally attend their first year of school, her mother worked part-time.

Tor watched as Melda rolled a shell between her fingers,

her head somewhere else. It was strange, but during their daily meetings, they didn't say much.

Mostly, Tor used the time to think.

And regret.

Last week, he had sprouted his first new emblem. It happened in the middle of the night. He awoke screaming at the top of his lungs, feeling like someone was carving at his arm with a butcher knife, then scrubbing it with sea salt. His father held him down while his mother took Rosa, who looked wide-eyed and frightened at his door, back to her room. His sister still didn't know what he was. And neither did anyone else in the village, other than his friends' parents.

He now only wore long-sleeved shirts that covered his arm, and his wrist, where his leadership marks once sat. Even on sweltering days like these.

There was one silver lining—in the month since they had returned, Tor hadn't heard from Queen Aurelia. Jeremiah somehow must have known that he had held up his end of the bargain.

"How does it feel?" Engle asked. His eyes were trained on the water, and Tor wondered how far he could see. "To get what you wanted for so long?"

Tor lifted his sleeve and looked at his arm, at the symbol of a fish. The emblem for water-breathing.

"Not like I expected," he said.

Engle nodded. "Figured." Then, he got up. "You know what I miss? From our journey?"

Melda smirked. "What? The child-eating old lady? Or, let me guess, the bonesulkers that almost killed you?"

Engle shuddered. "No, nothing *that* specific." He sighed "I miss the adventure."

Tor rubbed his eyes, itchy with exhaustion. Though it had been weeks, even thinking about their trip still sent a chill up his spine. Ever since the day he'd faced the Night Witch, he'd had nightmares. He replayed the events, over and over in his dreams, reliving what had happened on the cliff. Wondering if he could have done anything differently.

Melda groaned. "I, for one, will be happy if I never have to leave this village again."

"Okay, *Grim*elda."

She stuck her tongue out at him.

"Here's to *more* adventure," Engle challenged, holding his hand out, lifeline up. It had grown significantly after the Night Witch had removed their curse. All of theirs had. And the shapes were new, not the ones they had worn before Eve.

Strangely, their three lifelines now looked almost the same.

Melda made a show of exhaling deeply, then finally said, "To adventure," touching her lifeline to his.

Before Tor could join, something caught his eye. There was a large object floating on the water yards away, tucked between the waves.

"Tor?"

He didn't answer.

"Tor?"

"Engle, do you see that?"

Instead of replying, his friend took one look at the horizon, then rushed into the ocean, saltwater to his ankles. Tor, then Melda, followed.

No one said a word as the object Tor had spotted drifted closer and closer, sloshing with the current. Several minutes later it finally washed ashore, and Tor saw that it wasn't an object at all—but a person. A girl.

Tor crouched down, wondering if she was dead. That was when he saw it—an emblem on her wrist. That of a fish. He pressed a careful hand against her arm.

At once, her green eyes flew open. They were bloodshot. She looked scared, her face white as bone—her skin cold as a corpse. She said just two words before her eyes rolled back and her head fell against the sand.

"They're coming."

ACKNOWLEDGMENTS

Emblem Island would have lived forever in my mind and on my computer if it weren't for those who believed it should be printed and bound. Thank you to my incredible agent, Laura Bradford, who championed this story when it was a shadow of itself. To my amazing editor, Annie Berger, whose editorial magic is unmatched and whose suggestion to write more stories for *The Book of Cuentos* changed everything. To Sourcebooks, the best publisher I could have ever asked for. To Heather Moore—who must have a marketing emblem— Margaret Coffee, Michael Leali, Ashlyn Keil, Sarah Kasman, and Cassie Gutman.

Thank you to my parents, Keith and Claudy, who made it possible for me to chase this wild dream and raised me to believe I could do anything (look, Mom and Dad, we did it!).

Mom, you taught me to be strong. Dad, you taught me to be brave. To my twin sister/other half, Danny, who has read my books since we were thirteen, and whose opinion has always meant everything. To Rron, my heart, whose constant love and support has kept me resilient. To my early reader, Sean. To JonCarlos and Luna, my star and moon—this is for you. I hope you chase your wildest dreams. To Angely, who always says the right thing and is there when I need her. To Carlos, Alfonso, Maureen, and Julio for your never-wavering belief in me. To UPenn, where I blossomed into who I am. To my abuela, Rosenda, whose *cuentos* sparked my love of story-telling. To the Latin American stories that inspired this one: "La patasola," "La ciguapa," "La llorona," and "La niña con la estrella en la frente."

And to you, reader—because I am nothing without you.

ABOUT THE AUTHOR

Alex Aster recently graduated from the University of Pennsylvania, where she majored in English with a concentration in creative writing. The Emblem Island series is inspired by the Latin American myths her Colombian grandmother told her as a child before bedtime. She lives in New York. Explore the world of Emblem Island at asterverse.com.